Ashcroft:
The Fairy Queen &
The Dragon

by:

Alice Michelle Hook

Fox Fire Publications, LLC 2020
First book of the Ashcroft Forest Series

<u>Acknowledgements</u>

To my real life "Edie" for inspiring me to begin this adventure 12 years ago. To my real life "Jay": here's to our official 10 years. To my "Joe" and "Jordi", I love you both so much. I can't wait to read this with you. To "Queen Sharon", "Walt", "Wayne", and "Trista", thank you for continuing to be the biggest role models in my life. Thank you for always being encouraging and keeping me on the right track. To the real Joneé and Brendon for being adoptive parents to me for life. To my parents for listening to this story for over ten years. To my grandmother for giving me a typewriter and a love for writing. To my granny and poppa for showing me all manner of fairy tales. To Dr. Clark for recognizing and encouraging my love of writing and editing. And to TJ Berry for walking with me on this publishing journey! Thank you!

Fox Fire Publications would like to thank www.SelfPubBookCovers.com/ ACBookCovers for this amazing cover.

The Fairy Queen & The Dragon

Chapter One

Michael

"Edie! Wake up!" Abbie said, gently shaking Edie's shoulders.

"What is it, Abbie?" Edie asked, groggily. "Did you have a bad dream?"

"No, Edie," Abbie responded. "There's a new sprite in the Ashcroft Forest!"

Edie rolled over defiantly and pulled her woven blanket over her head. "Go back to bed, Abbie! There hasn't been a new sprite to the village for ages!"

"Edie, get up! There really is a new sprite," Abbie persisted. "Joneé told me his name was Michael. Let's go meet him."

When Edie still did not roll over, Abbie pulled the long curtains she had made for Edie back from the small window in her bedroom.

Edie shielded her face from the light for a moment, but then understood that she wasn't dreaming. "Now get dressed so that we can make some cookies to take to him," Abbie said.

As Abbie waited for Edie to get dressed, she looked at the hand drawn art on Edie's wall. Drawing pictures was Edie's favorite thing to do. She always had something with her to draw on so that she could stop and draw whatever she saw.

Abbie looked at her favorite one, the drawing that Edie had done of the two of them. She thought Edie had done a marvelous job on her self-portrait though Edie said she liked how she had drawn Abbie better. Edie was just over six feet tall, and she was thin. She had long willowy brown hair, and Abbie thought she had nicely done her own sky-blue eyes. She had even used the same blue to color her matching wings.

Abbie looked at herself in the drawing. She was slightly shorter than Edie was and had long chestnut hair and dark brown eyes. Her wings had a light purple tint. Abbie liked the way her hair looked, tossed by the wind.

Her thoughts were interrupted by Edie emerging from the bedroom. Edie shook her head when she saw what Abbie was looking at. "Come on, Abbie," she said. "Let's go make those cookies."

They headed over to Abbie's house since Abbie had most of the supplies for baking. Edie's kitchen had a few carved animals on the counter and had the basics of cookware. She lacked some of the fancier tools for cooking that Abbie had. Edie was better at cooking things like soups and frying vegetables, whereas Abbie was better at baking breads and sweet treats.

Abbie and Edie were nearly inseparable. No matter what they were doing, they were almost always together. They gathered food together, ate together, went to social gatherings and parties together, and did work like cleaning their houses together. They lived across the path from each other. The only time they seemed to spend apart was when they were asleep.

The two of them baked the nut and berry cookies that were Abbie's specialty. Then they went over to the guest house where Joneé had told Abbie Michael would be staying. The village that the sprites of the Ashcroft Forest lived in was quaint. Their houses were built amongst the mighty oaks that dominated the forest. The houses were made out of wood, but each had a distinctive flair that reflected its owner. The two talented sprites who built the houses, Wayne and Walt, put a lot of time and detail into their work. Besides houses, the village also had the other necessary buildings like a meeting hall and a healing room for sick sprites.

When they reached the house, it took them a moment to remember where the front door was as the forest had reclaimed the house and covered it liberally in ivy. Abbie finally found the large, slender front door and parted the curtain of ivy so that they could knock on it. The sprite who answered the door was a tall, rather handsome young sprite with very short brown hair and ruggedly blue eyes. His wings were glittering silver in color.

He answered the door wearing an olive-green tunic with brown pants that came to just above his ankles. He wasn't wearing any shoes, but Edie noticed a pair of small flat shoes just inside the door.

"Hi! We're Abbie and Edie, and we'd like to welcome you to the community," Edie said. "Abbie and I baked these cookies for you as a welcome present."

"Well that's so thoughtful of you. I appreciate it," Michael replied a bit shyly. "I'm Michael." He took the cookies from them with a slight smile. He looked down at his bare feet before looking back up at them. "I'd ask you to come in, but I'm still getting settled into my house."

"That's OK," Abbie said. "We've got to be going anyway. It was nice to meet you though, Michael."

"Nice to meet you too. Have a good day," Michael answered.

"You too. See you at the party tonight," Abbie added. Michael nodded like he wasn't sure what they meant before he shut the door.

Sprites love any reason to celebrate (they even celebrate the 8th of the month). So that night there was a big welcome celebration for Michael. There was much food, dancing, and music. Abbie sang a new song that she had written. She wore a purple flowing dress that she had decorated with fresh flowers that she and Edie had picked together. The festivities lasted long into the night.

After all of the frivolities of the previous night, the sprites of the Ashcroft Forest slept late the next day. Sprites are interesting creatures. They do most everything for themselves, such as gathering and preparing food or making their own clothes. Sprites are social and enjoy celebrations, gatherings, and sharing meals. Sprites don't have jobs where they make money, but each one plays a role in the community. Edie was the Ashcroft Forest's best artist, and she loved to help with odd projects around the village. Abbie's main role in the Ashcroft Forest was to write and entertain the sprites at different functions. She also enjoyed growing and harvesting her own food. Abbie, like Edie, loved to pitch in and help the other sprites with odd jobs.

When Abbie woke up the next afternoon, she decided to go over to Edie's house to help her clean her house. She pulled on a loose black top that had a large opening in the back for her wings and had a small, thin strap that clasped at the base of her neck. Abbie selected a loose brown skirt that she had made herself and sewn pockets into to make it more practical. She slid on black slippers that encased her feet and headed over to Edie's house.

Edie wasn't awake yet when Abbie got there, so Abbie headed home to practice one of the new songs she had been writing. On her way back, she spotted Michael working on the exterior of the house he was living in. Being the friendly sprite she was, Abbie decided to walk over and see if she could help him.

"How's it going today, Michael?" she asked.

"It's going pretty well," he answered. "I had fun last night, but I'm trying to work on getting my house set up now."

"Is this where you're going to be living permanently?" Abbie asked. "Or are they going to build you your own house?"

"I'm not sure," Michael said. "But until I decide, I will make this place feel more like mine."

"Can I help?" Abbie asked.

"Sure," Michael replied.

The two of them looked at the exterior and gave a collective sigh. The ivy covered almost all of the exterior, so that had to be carefully cleared. This took some time, but when they finished with that, the two of them went inside. The interior had also been untouched, so the two of them worked together to clean and sweep the inside of the house.

The house Michael was in was a one-story house with a living room, kitchen, and small bedroom. The rooms had sparse but adequate furniture. They cleaned the interior of the house, and Abbie picked some fresh flowers to make it feel a bit more like home.

Michael invited Abbie to stay for dinner. He didn't have much as far as food since he had just arrived, but the community had already made sure that he was set up with enough until he could begin growing and gathering his own food. Abbie helped him put together a salad from what he had, and the two of them had a nice meal. After dinner, the two of them sat and talked for a long time. It was starting to get dark when Abbie finally headed back to her house.

The next morning, Edie went over to Abbie's house to gather food together as the two of them usually did. "Abbie! I'm glad to see that you're OK," Edie said, sounding relieved. "Are you ready to go?"

"I'm all set. I invited Michael to go with us, too. I hope that's alright," she added.

"Of course," Edie said. She and Abbie walked next-door and told Michael that they were ready to leave. The three of them set off to gather food. It didn't take long for the subject of the previous day to come up.

"That mushroom looks like the little cluster of mushrooms that were growing in the front corner of your house," Abbie said pointing and laughing.

"You're right," Michael said, joining her laughter.

The more Abbie and Michael talked, Abbie observed, the quieter Edie got. Edie could feel a jealousy welling inside her and her face getting hot, but she wasn't quite sure where it came from. She kept her eyes down and tried to avoid looking at the other two. When they returned to the village, and Michael went into his house, Abbie asked Edie what was wrong.

"I was worried about you when I couldn't find you yesterday, but apparently you were off with your new friend," Edie said, rolling her eyes. She tried hard not to let her temper get the best of her, and she knew she was letting it show. She took a deep breath before she said something she regretted.

"Edie, I was just trying to be nice to him and be a friend to him. He's new here and doesn't know anyone," Abbie defended.

"Well I guess that's OK," Edie conceded sheepishly, her anger subsiding. "But I was really worried about you! I thought something had happened to you!"

"I'm sorry I worried you like that. I'll be more careful to let you know where I am," Abbie apologized.

"It's alright," Edie replied.

Edie returned to her house, still feeling a little resentful over the situation, but she resolved herself to let it go.

~~~

That night Abbie went over to Edie's house for dinner. Edie's house was like a small log cabin on the first floor. She had a small kitchen, bedroom, and sitting room. The second floor of her home was completely open except for a railing that came waist high. It served as Edie's art studio. There was a small stool and an easel that Edie moved depending on the time of day.

Edie's house was more decorated to suit her personality. Her dining room table had only two chairs because it was usually just her and Abbie having dinner. She had a sitting area with two chairs and a couch, where she and Abbie had shared many cups
~~~

of tea. The two of them had just started cooking their vegetables for dinner when there was a knock at the door.

"Oh, that'll be Michael," Abbie said nonchalantly.

"Oh, I see," said Edie, trying to hide her disappointment. She felt bitterness rising in her from earlier. She tried to push it away again, telling herself it wasn't justified.

However, Abbie wouldn't have seen any of the displeasure on Edie's face anyway, because she was already opening the door to let Michael into the house. Edie went into her bedroom and took the chair from her room to sit in so that Michael could have a kitchen chair. She sighed to herself but decided not to make a big deal in front of the others.

Michael was grateful to have someone to share dinner with and thanked the sprites profusely for letting him come over. Although Edie was upset at first that Michael had come over, she realized by the end of the night that he was quite nice.

The next morning, Edie got up early and went out to one of the fields to draw for a while. When Abbie went over to Edie's house, she was gone. Abbie wondered where Edie was and debated whether or not to go look for Edie. Abbie saw that Michael was working outside his house. She decided to go look for Edie after she talked to Michael.

"What's the project for today?" Abbie asked him.

"I'm trying to rake the leaves and pull up weeds so that I can plant a garden," he told her.

Abbie offered her help, and the two began the work. When Edie returned for lunch, she saw Abbie out working with Michael. She was suddenly oozing with jealousy. About that time, Abbie noticed Edie had come home. Abbie ran over to greet her. When Abbie got closer though, she saw that Edie was upset.

"What's wrong, Edie?" asked Abbie.

"What's wrong?" Edie repeated. "What's wrong is that I've lost my best friend! This guy moves in, and all of the sudden you're only interested in being with him! We can't do anything without having him there! Every time I look for you, you're over at his house! I can't believe that you would trade our friendship like this! Next thing I know, you'll have moved in with him or something!"

"Edie, what are you talking about?" a surprised Abbie sputtered.

"I thought you were my friend. But I guess I was wrong!" Edie choked, kicking the pebble closest to her foot.

"Edie, wait!" Abbie called, but Edie didn't want to listen. Edie ran to her house and slammed the door before anyone could see her cry.

Abbie tried hard over the next several days to restore her friendship with Edie. However, Edie refused to listen to anything she said. Edie wouldn't even open the door to Abbie. If she saw Abbie outside, she'd hurry into her house without so much as a word. So, Abbie ended up spending more and more time with Michael. Seeing Abbie and Michael together just made Edie more jealous than ever. Any time she saw either one of them walking her way, she would turn and go the other direction. Edie made sure that she went to different places to gather her food. She felt like a part of her soul had been ripped out. Edie just couldn't understand why Abbie would betray their friendship like this.

Abbie was confused by the incident. She knew that Edie stayed mostly to herself when she wasn't with Abbie. Abbie knew that she was just trying to make Michael feel at home. Why couldn't Edie understand that? There was no way that she would ever want Edie to feel left out.

On the other hand, Abbie was really enjoying getting to know Michael. Although he was shy to begin with, once she got to know him, he was very fun to be around. The story of how he came to the Ashcroft Forest was very interesting. Michael had grown up with the group of sprites that lived in the Dixon Glade. A few weeks ago though, he had woken up in the middle of a clearing just a short distance from the Dixon Glade. When Michael went back to his village, everyone was gone. The entire village was deserted. He decided the best thing to do was to set off on his own in search of shelter. On his second day of traveling, he came across a sparrow who told him about a little sprite community that he knew of. The sparrow gave Michael directions of how to get there. After two days travel, he had arrived at the sprite village in the Ashcroft Forest. Michael had gone to Fen, the village leader and told him of his plight. The wise old leader had welcomed him with open arms.

The gap in Michael's memory worried him. He knew that something important had happened to his family and friends during that time, but he just couldn't remember what. Michael hoped that someday his memory would eventually come back to him. He told himself that if his memories ever did return, he would search everywhere until he found his lost tribe.

Although Michael was very sad to have lost his family, he was glad that he had found friendship with Abbie. He was just sorry that somehow the fact that Abbie was friends with him had shattered the friendship between Abbie and Edie. Michael could tell that Abbie really missed Edie and that it hurt her when Edie avoided her. So, he decided to see what he could do to reconcile their relationship.

Michael went to the wisest female sprite in the Ashcroft tribe, Joneé. Joneé was one of the kindest sprites in the tribe. She shared the responsibilities of leading the sprites with Fen. She loved to talk with people and give advice. Michael figured that she might be able to tell him what to do. Joneé came through with some great advice for Michael to use. Joneé suggested that Michael try to talk to Edie by himself and explain to her what was going on and how much Abbie missed her.

So that night, Michael asked Edie to come over to his house for dinner. After a lot of persuading, Edie reluctantly agreed. Edie had been very lonely and angry the past few days. She couldn't understand why Abbie would want to spend her time with Michael rather than her. Abbie had been her best friend since they were little sprites. Abbie was the one person she felt she could confide in, and Edie felt abandoned. She did not want to go and have dinner with Michael, but he was very persuasive.

Edie reluctantly got ready and went over to Michael's house. She thought about dressing up but decided that she wanted to be more comfortable. Although she was very polite, Michael could see that she was extremely uncomfortable. She kept looking at her plate rather than at Michael. After they got past a few pleasantries about the weather and a few things like that, Michael decided to get straight to the point.

"Edie, why are you so upset with Abbie?" he asked.

Edie sat there for a moment, seeming shocked at the forwardness of his question. She poked at her food and shifted her jaw tensely. After a moment she said, "Because when you came along, the two of you became inseparable, and I knew I was losing my best friend. I can't believe she would betray our friendship! I can't believe that she would just abandon me!"

"Edie," Michael began gently. She opened her mouth as if she was going to interrupt him, but he held up a hand to continue. Edie pursed her lips and folded her arms impatiently, but she let him continue. "Let me start off by letting you now that there is nothing romantic going on between us," he said. "When I moved in, Abbie realized that I needed a friend. And she was right. I was very lonely when I got here. Abbie became my friend when I needed one."

Then he told Edie the story of how he had come to the Ashcroft Forest. Michael was silent for a minute after he finished his story. He could tell that Edie was taking all of it in.

Then he continued, "I know for a fact though, that Abbie would never abandon you. She's missed you a lot. I bet if you go talk to her, the two of you can work it out."

Edie's eyes glittered with tears. "Thank you for talking to me, Michael. Do you mind if I go talk to her right now?" she asked impulsively.

"Of course," Michael said gladly.

"I'll be right back," said Edie.

Edie got up from the table and hugged Michael who was quite shocked by the gesture. Then she sprinted over to Abbie's house. She walked up to the house and then knocked on the door.

"Abbie?" she called rather timidly.

"Yes? Is that you Edie?" Edie heard Abbie yell from the back of her house.

"Yes, Abbie. It's Edie," she replied.

Edie heard footsteps running toward the door. Abbie opened the door looking slightly flustered.

"What's going on Edie? Are you alright?" Abbie asked frantically. Her hands were covered in flour, probably from baking some bread.

"I'm fine," Edie said. "I just wanted to tell you how sorry I am about what's happened lately. I didn't mean to jump to conclusions, but I got so jealous when I saw you hanging around Michael all the time. I just didn't want to lose you as a friend. I think I went about it the wrong way though. I talked to Michael, and I want to be friends with both of you. He's a nice guy, and I'd like to have you both as friends. So, I guess the main question is: will you forgive me, Abbie?"

"Of course, I will, Edie!" Abbie exclaimed as she hugged Edie, careful not to get flour on her back. "That's what I'd been hoping for all along! I befriended Michael because I knew he was lonely, not because I didn't want to be your friend anymore."

"Let's go back over to Michael's house," suggested Edie. "He fixed dinner for me, and I bet we can find something over there for you."

Abbie finished kneading her bread and left it to rise. What she didn't know was that Michael had hoped that Edie and Abbie would patch things up, so he had fixed an extra portion for Abbie just in case. So, Michael was very excited when Edie brought Abbie with her. From that day on, Edie, Abbie, and Michael were all good friends. Little did they know that this was just the beginning of their adventures.

Chapter Two

The Fox

It was a beautifully clear summer night. Edie decided to go out into the field and sketch the moon. Since it was warm, she didn't bother to get a sweater or sleeves like she normally would. She glided silently through the night. She found a rock to sit on and began to sketch. Suddenly, Edie heard a noise behind her. At first, she thought it was the wind and paid it no heed, but then she felt an intense pinch of pain in her shoulder, like something had stung her. However, when Edie turned around, no one was there. There was no bug, no bee, nothing at all. A bit frightened, she quickly gathered her things and headed back to her house.

Once Edie got home, she quickly went to the full-length mirror in her room. She checked the spot on her shoulder to see if there was any mark there above the top of her corset. Her skin was as milky white as ever, and there was no visible scar or bump. She scolded herself for being so jumpy. There was nothing to be scared about at all.

The next morning, Edie awoke to hear a commotion outside. She quickly dressed and then walked outside. She caught herself glancing at her shoulder in the mirror before she left her bedroom. Her skin still showed no mark or any sign of damage.

Edie could hear the noise coming from behind Catey's house, where the village apple orchard was. When Catey's backyard came into view, she could see it was littered with apples. She gasped at the sight of several almost bare trees in the middle of the growing season. When she came closer, she could see the apples were mostly untouched, but some had large bites taken out of them or had been crushed. The bites looked like they had been taken by an animal.

Catey was sitting on her back porch, sobbing. Catey was a sprite about Edie's height with black hair, flaming red wings, and stormy green eyes. Edie felt bad for her because she knew how much care Catey put into tending her trees. Joneé and a few other sprites were sitting and talking to her, trying to get her to calm down. Several other sprites were cleaning up the scattered apples. She saw Abbie and Michael picking up apple cores and putting them into a basket, so she walked over to see if they knew what had happened.

Things had been going better between Edie and Michael. They were starting to be rather good friends. Edie, Michael, and Abbie hung out together on a regular basis.

"What happened?" Edie asked the two of them when she got closer.

"Catey said she heard something last night, but when she went out to check on it, nothing was there. Then when she got up this morning, she saw all of the apples littering her yard," Abbie explained.

"So, no one knows what did this?" Edie asked.

"No, not yet. But I'm sure Fen will figure out what it was," Michael replied, brushing some leaves out of Abbie's long, toffee-colored hair. Abbie wiped her hands on the folds of her skirt before standing.

"We're sorting these apples into the whole ones that can be stored temporarily, the apples that can have small bites out of them so we can cut that off and use the rest of the apples, and the cores that can be used for seeds," Abbie told Edie. "Grab a basket and help Michael and me."

The sprites soon got the mess cleaned up, and everyone went back to their usual activities. The next day was the eighth of the month, so everyone was preparing for their monthly celebration. Michael couldn't wait for the celebration. Since he had been in the Ashcroft Forest, he had heard about these celebrations. The sprites always had a lot of singing, dancing, food, and fun at these parties. Fen had asked Michael to tell everyone a story about his life in the Dixon Glade. He couldn't wait until the next evening.

The rest of the day passed in a flurry of activity with everyone preparing food and decorations for the party. When Edie got home that night, she was dreadfully tired. She slept long and hard that night. She felt like she was coming out of a fog when she was awakened the next morning by a knock on the door.

"Edie!" Abbie called. "Edie, come out here!"

Edie hurriedly pulled on some dark leggings and an off-white shirt and rushed to the door.

"What is it Abbie?" Edie asked with concern.

"It's Michael. Something got into his house, and there's food all over the kitchen," Abbie said.

"Well, let's go over there and see how we can help," Edie said stepping out the door.

They walked the short distance from Edie's house to Michael's house. From the outside, Michael's house looked normal. It looked just like it had the day before. However, the inside of the house looked like a disaster. Some kind of creature had gotten into Michael's house. It looked like the same thing that had destroyed Catey's garden had gotten into Michael's house. However, it had somehow opened the outside door. There was food everywhere. A trail of half-eaten food led from the front door to the kitchen. The trail ended below a shelf where Michael had stored his fruits and vegetables. Michael was on the floor trying to mop up a big puddle of sticky, nasty goop just below the shelves. Abbie and Edie immediately pitched in to help Michael clean.

"What happened, Michael?" Edie asked.

"Apparently I had a visitor last night," Michael replied, stopping for a second to wipe his brow.

"Didn't you hear anything?" Abbie asked.

"I heard a commotion this morning, and this is what I found when I got up to investigate. I heard whatever made this mess running out the door when I got up," he sighed.

"I'm going to get Fen so that he can see the damage before we clean up all the evidence," said Abbie.

"Alright. That's probably a good idea," Michael and Edie replied.

Edie and Michael stopped cleaning and waited for Abbie to return with Fen. Edie sat down in one of Michael's kitchen chairs. Michael looked through his remaining food and found a butternut squash and some honey for them to share for breakfast.

The two of them ate together in mostly silence, but it wasn't the awkward silence it would have been a short time before. This was more to let Michael process what happened.

"You know what's strange, Edie?" Michael asked as he finished eating his breakfast.

"What?" Edie returned.

"Whatever raided my cabinet didn't bother any of my vegetables," he said.

Edie looked over at the goop on the floor and canted her head when she saw a cucumber in the middle of the mess.

Michael followed her line of sight. "Oh, the cucumber?" he asked, holding up the dripping vegetable. "It's whole," he said, turning it around. "But all of my apples and berries are gone."

They looked at each other in silence, each not knowing what to do with that information.

It didn't take long for Abbie to come back with Fen. He quickly assessed the damage.

"Well, I'm not sure what this creature is, but I think we should call a conference. We have to find a way to stop whatever this is and make sure that it doesn't ruin the celebration tonight. I'll go let everyone know," Fen said.

Fen left to notify the rest of the sprites about the meeting. Edie, Michael, and Abbie stayed and finished cleaning up Michael's house. Then they walked over to the meeting hall where the conference was about to begin.

Fen and Joneé, the two leaders of the sprites, sat on the platform at the front of the room. The two created quite a contrast. Fen commanded attention by being the tallest sprite in the Ashcroft Forest and having yellow wings, pearly white skin, and a hairless head. Joneé on the other hand, was a bit shorter with creamy bister-colored skin, short raven hair, and deep purple wings. Fen started the meeting soon after Edie, Michael, and Abbie sat down. All of the sprites who lived in the Ashcroft Forest had shown up for the conference.

"As I told each of you when I talked to you earlier, our nighttime visitor has struck again," Fen began. "What we need to do is figure out a plan of how to stop this creature from breaking in and eating our food."

"Why don't we trap it and kill it?" suggested a young sprite named Joe.

"Do we really need to kill it?" asked Edie.

"I like the idea of setting a trap. But I don't think we have to kill it," said Joneé. "I think if a few of us volunteer to guard the village, just for an hour or so, then we can capture it and see what it is."

"I could make something that could trap the creature and not harm it," volunteered Walt, who was the town's carpenter. He was a rather tall sprite with grassy green wings, gray hair, and dark eyes.

"I like Joneé's idea, but what about the celebration tonight?" asked Abbie.

"If we volunteer in pairs for an hour each, then we'll only miss an hour of the celebration. Our only other options are to cancel the celebration or to allow for the possibility that the vandal might strike again," Fen reasoned.

"Then I say we go with Joneé's idea," Catey said.

The assembled sprites took a vote and unanimously approved Joneé's plan. Fen passed around a piece of paper, and everyone signed up in pairs to keep watch that night. As soon as each sprite signed up for a time, he or she scampered off to finish their preparations for that night's festivities. Edie and Abbie took the first watch. Although Abbie wasn't frightened about encountering the creature, Edie was a bit apprehensive. Their watch turned out to be quite uneventful, however. After an hour, Fen and Joe came to take over. Edie was exhausted. Although she wanted to go to the celebration, she decided to go back to her house and get some sleep.

Abbie, however, headed to the celebration. She arrived just in time to hear Michael begin his storytelling.

"My life in the Dixon Glade was not much different from yours here. Our homes were set around the glade on the edge of the forest that stretches between here and there. We frequently had deer and elk come through our village. There were twenty-five of us living in the Dixon Glade. My best friend was a sprite named Jay. He was the village 'fixer' as we called him. He could work on anything, mechanical or not and get it running again."

Michael trailed off and stared at the top of the tree line. Abbie turned to look in the direction he was. Joe flew into the clearing.

"We've found something! We've found something!" the excited young sprite cried.

After Joe calmed down, the waiting sprites were able to get him to tell them what had occurred. While on patrol, Fen and Joe had caught a fox eating some of the berries outside of Walt's house. The two of them had captured it and put it in a cage. Fen was standing watch while Joe flew to tell the rest of them. The sprites quickly packed up their things from the festivities and headed back to the village to see the fox. When they arrived in the village, they saw Fen standing next to the cage that held a fox with beautiful copper colored fur.

"Aw, it was just a little hungry fox," said Joneé.

"But it's good that we caught it," said Fen. "Now it won't bother us anymore."

"What are we going to do with it?" asked Catey.

"It's too late to decide anything tonight," Fen said. "We'll figure that out in the morning. Sorry we had to interrupt your story, Michael. You'll finish it another night, I hope?"

"Absolutely," Michael replied.

"Good. Abbie, will you take care of breakfast for the fox in the morning?" Fen asked.

"Yes, I will," Abbie agreed.

"Alright. We'll move the fox into the meeting hall for now," Fen said.

Several of the sprites helped Fen transport the fox in the cage into the hall. The rest of the sprites headed home after a night of celebration.

When Abbie woke up the next morning, she realized that Edie had gone home early and missed all of the excitement with the fox. She decided to go tell her after she took breakfast to the furry bandit. Now knowing that the thief was a fox made sense as to why it only disturbed the berries and apples. However, Abbie was surprised that it had stayed so long in the Ashcroft Forest and hadn't left to get meat.

Abbie put on a light blue halter top that came down and tied in a bow under her wings. She put on a white skirt to go along with it, and she put on slippers. Abbie fixed a bowl of berries, walked over to the meeting hall, and opened the door.

Abbie heard the animal stir slightly as she shut the door behind her. She began humming as she walked toward the cage to let the animal know she was there. Abbie looked into the cage and jumped back out of fear, almost dropping the bowl she was carrying. Instead of a fox lying in front of her in a cage, she saw Edie lying in the cage fully clothed. Edie wasn't known for sleep walking, so Abbie was confused as to why she was there.

"Edie?" she asked when she had regained her voice.

Edie looked up at her, confused. She took in her surroundings, and her eyes grew wide with fear.

"Abbie? What am I doing in a cage?" Edie asked, gripping the bars as best she could, her voice trembling with fright.

"We caught a fox in that cage last night! Where did you take it?" rebutted Abbie in a breathless voice.

"A fox? What are you talking about? Who put me in this cage?" asked Edie. Her eyes narrowed. "Is this some kind of joke?"

"You mean you didn't let the fox go?" asked a confused Abbie.

"What fox?!" exclaimed Edie angrily. "Let me out of here!"

"Oh no, Edie," said Abbie.

"What?" asked Edie again.

"Well, if you didn't let the fox out..." Abbie paused for a second, trying to make sure she worded it correctly but frustrating Edie.

"Abbie, please finish your statement," Edie demanded through clenched teeth.

"Well, if you didn't let the fox out...then maybe you...are the fox..." Abbie stammered.

"What are you talking about, you crazy sprite?" Edie asked nervously.

"Let me go get Fen and Joneé. I'll be right back," said Abbie.

"Abbie, wait!" Edie demanded. "Let me out of here!" But she was too late because Abbie had already rushed out.

While she was gone, Edie mulled over the situation. She was crammed into a cage that was clearly made for a much smaller creature. The last few nights she had gone home and slept peacefully. Or at least she thought she had. Nevertheless, Edie knew that she had felt unnaturally tired the last two days. And her thoughts suddenly turned to the night in the forest when she was sketching the moon.

The realization of what had happened hit her hard. She must have had a spell cast on her with that sting she felt on her shoulder. Her stomach dropped. She began to weep in the cage while she waited for Abbie to come back. Her head leaned forward until it was resting on the leg of her trousers. She laughed to herself between gulps of air when she realized how thankful she was that the spell did not make her naked when she changed back into her sprite form.

When Fen and Joneé arrived, Edie poured out the whole story between sobs. They both listened to her and thought for a moment.

"It sounds like a fairy spell," Joneé said. "We'll have to send you to the fairies to see if they can undo it. Do you know where the closest fairies live, Fen?"

"There's a band of fairies that live by Holli Lake," Fen answered. "We'll have to prepare you to journey there."

Fen then let her out of the cage. Fen and Joneé decided that while they were getting Edie ready for her journey that they would lock her in her house every night to make sure that she didn't hurt anyone or destroy any more property. The sprites got busy preparing for Edie's trip. Edie would need food to eat, though she could gather some on the way. She would also need a present for the fairies, and something to hopefully use to barter for a cure.

Edie was miserable with the stress of the upcoming quest. She knew that it was going to be a long hard journey, and she was not looking forward to it. Seeing how much pain Edie was going though, Abbie and Michael discussed with Fen the possibility of the two of them going with Edie on her quest. After a bit of persuading, Fen agreed to let Abbie and Michael go with Edie. When Michael and Abbie told Edie that they would be accompanying her, she almost wept with happiness. It made her feel so much better to know that her friends were going to go with her on this expedition.

Chapter Three

The Journey

Only four days had passed since Edie had decided to travel to visit the fairies, but they had gone quickly. During the day, Edie, Michael, and Abbie had gotten a plan together, gathered food, and made presents for the fairies.

At night, Edie would turn into a fox. Although Abbie was supposed to be guarding Edie in her house, she discovered that Edie the fox was responsive to her. She felt bad about keeping her cooped up in the house, so Abbie would sneak her out to explore. She kept a watchful eye on her during these times, so she didn't destroy anything else. Edie was beginning to remember these nighttime adventures better and was starting to be able to control some of her behavior. Edie was actually starting to enjoy being a fox.

Abbie would make sure that she got Edie back into her house before the sun rose. She was just glad that Edie would turn back into herself fully clothed.

On that fourth morning, Edie got up, got dressed, packed her sweater, and checked the contents of her bag. A few minutes later, Abbie and Michael knocked on her door. Both of them had everything with them that they needed for the journey so the three of them set off for the edge of the village. Fen and Joneé were waiting for them when the three friends reached the village gate.

"Take care while you're gone," Joneé said as she hugged each of them.

"We will," Michael, Abbie, and Edie all agreed.

Fen gave them a few last-minute instructions before they left. It would be about a three-day journey by flight to Holli Lake. The three sprites would fly as much as they could during the day and then sleep at night. Since Edie was able to control her fox instincts better, Michael and Abbie didn't have to worry about her running off at night or destroying anything while they were asleep. Fen gave Abbie a knowing look that she knew meant he knew about their night time excursions.

Abbie's father, Rufus, came up as the sprites were saying goodbye to Fen and Joneé. "Be careful," he said to her as he hugged her. He didn't need to say more. She knew that he also meant he was proud of her bravery but concerned about what he knew might lay ahead for them.

"I will, dad," she said.

He joined Joneé and Fen, and the three of them watched the three young sprites fly off on their journey.

After about an hour of flying, the sprites took a break to eat. Abbie had made some apple jam sandwiches for them made from the apples Edie as a fox had plucked from the trees. While they were eating, Edie suddenly realized that Abbie was studying her intently.

"What's wrong?" Edie asked.

"Did you do something to your hair last night?" Abbie asked her.

"No, I haven't. Why?" replied Edie, fingering a strand of her long, flowing hair.

"Your hair has a copper tint to it today. I didn't know if it was the sun, or you'd washed it differently, or..." her voice trailed off.

"Or what?" asked Edie nervously.

"Or...if the spell was getting a stronger hold on you and changing your hair to the color of fox fur," Abbie begrudgingly answered.

"Oh," said Edie, the pit of her stomach once again dropping. She guessed she should have realized that this spell would not only turn her into a fox at night but would also slowly take her over until she was a fox completely. The only question was, how long would it be before the spell was complete? Only time could tell, and she was glad that they were only two days away from Holli Lake.

Edie, Abbie, and Michael soon finished their meal and were on their way again. Even though the noise of the wind rushing past them made it impossible for the fairies to talk to one another, Edie was still glad that she wasn't alone. She tugged the sleeves of her sweater down closer to her hands. The wind was cold when they flew into it. When the wind wasn't in their faces, she could occasionally catch the tune Abbie was humming to herself. As she flew along, she thought about how lucky she was to have such good friends.

That night they camped under a cluster of oak trees. Michael, Abbie, and Edie all stretched out on the ground and were soon asleep. About an hour later, Edie woke up as a fox and began to explore the forest. Even though she had been through this part of the forest before, it all seemed new through her fox eyes. Her senses had grown very acute over the last few days. New, delicious smells surrounded her as she made her way through the trees. The cool night air felt refreshing as she sprinted through the forest.

After a few hours of exploring, Edie went back to the cluster of oak trees where Abbie and Michael were still sleeping. She curled up beside them and was soon asleep. It seemed to Edie that only a few minutes had elapsed before Abbie woke her up. Her back felt sore from sleeping on the ground. When Edie reached back to rub her back and wings, she felt something soft and furry behind her. She choked down her surprise at first, because she thought it was an animal. However, when she pulled the end of the tail around, she realized it was attached to her back. It was actually a beautiful red tail with a white tip.

She gasped with what she held in her hand, alerting the attention of Michael and Abbie. "What is that?!" Michael exclaimed.

He looked at Abbie, whose hand had snapped to her mouth. "The spell is taking more of her," Abbie said removing her hand to speak.

Even though she really liked her new tail, Edie was frightened by the fact that the spell was moving so quickly. The effects of the spell seemed to unnerve Abbie and Michael as well, so they decided to get on their way quickly. Edie remembered where some berry bushes were from her night time adventures. She showed them where they were, and the three of them ate quickly before setting off.

Flying was more awkward that day since Edie now had a tail. There certainly was no way of flying that was terribly graceful, so Edie quickly gave up on that and focused on staying in the air. Even though the sprites traveled slower that day than they had the first day, they realized that if things went about the same the next day, they would reach the fairies by the middle of the next afternoon.

The three of them made a small fire and roasted some vegetables for a modest meal from the little bit of food that they had left from home. Then they all stretched out on the forest floor and fell asleep. A little while later, Edie the fox awoke for her nighttime adventures. Edie had never been to this part of the forest before, so she enjoyed getting to explore all of the new things. A short time later, Edie returned to the spot where Michael and Abbie were. She sleepily curled up and drifted off to sleep.

The next morning, Abbie woke Edie up as she had so many mornings before. But this morning Edie could tell by the look on Abbie's face that something was wrong.

"What is it Abbie?" Edie asked.

Abbie hesitated for a second before she told her.

"Edie, I don't know how we're going to get to the fairies," Abbie said when she finally regained her voice.

"What do you mean?" Edie asked, standing up and looking between Abbie and Michael's worried faces.

"Well, you've got fox ears today Edie. But that's not really the worst of it," said Michael slowly.

"Then what's going on?" Edie demanded.

"Your wings have disappeared, Edie," Abbie choked.

Edie's hands immediately reached for her back. As soon as she touched her back, she knew that Abbie was telling the truth. Edie suddenly felt like she was going to cry. The whole quest seemed hopeless. If she couldn't fly, Edie didn't think there was any way they would make it to Holli Lake before she turned completely into a fox. Edie was on the verge of telling Michael and Abbie to go home and just abandon her when Abbie walked over and put her hand on Edie's shoulder.

"Don't worry Edie," Abbie said. "We'll just go on foot. It will take a little longer, but we'll still get there."

Edie was glad that Abbie had so much optimism. She really hoped that Abbie would be right. Michael, Edie, and Abbie got their supplies together and set off immediately. On their way through the forest, they picked some berries and ate them while they walked. The nice thing about walking was the fact that the three sprites could talk to each other. Although all three of the sprites were concerned for Edie's plight, they lightened the mood as best as they could by making jokes and telling humorous stories. Edie joked with the others that she was glad that Fen had recommended they wear sandals so that they weren't having to walk barefoot. None of them focused on the fact that their food had run out or the fact that they were all more hungry than they were used to.

Night loomed, and they still had a few hours of walking ahead of them before they could make it to Holli Lake. Michael, Abbie, and Edie were all exhausted from all of the walking they had done that day, so they decided to get a good night's sleep before they continued their journey. All three of them stretched out and were quickly asleep. Once again, Edie the fox was awake after about an hour. That night though, she didn't enjoy her explorations. Edie was consumed by the worry that she would have turned into a fox for good when she woke up the next morning. Finally, she went back to where Michael and Abbie were sleeping and fell into a troubled sleep beside them.

Morning came too soon for Edie. She was absolutely exhausted. Abbie and Michael were off about a yard away picking berries and mint for breakfast. She decided to walk over toward them to see if she could help. Abbie looked up at her as she approached and gave a small smile.

"Come down to the stream with me, Edie. Help me wash these berries," Abbie said simply. She took Edie's hand and turned toward the water. Edie allowed Abbie to lead her down to the stream. Edie thought that this was more than just the berries, and she felt her stomach drop. Neither of them said a word during their short walk. Just before they reached the bank, Abbie put up her hand.

"Edie, I wanted you to see this for yourself, but it may come as a shock. So just prepare yourself," Abbie said softly.

Edie walked to the bank of the small stream and gazed at her reflection. She immediately began to cry when she saw a fox's copper, furry face staring back at her from the water. Abbie knelt behind Edie and placed a hand on her shoulder while she cried. After a few minutes, Edie composed herself. The two sprites rejoined Michael, and they had a quiet meal.

It would be about a half-day's journey to Holli Lake. None of the sprites said much as they walked along. The occasional chirp of a bird seemed alien and eerie. Edie felt as though she had been walking for ages. Just when she thought she couldn't go any farther, they arrived at a small clearing in the forest. A few yards away they could see the glimmering surface of Holli Lake, framed by towering willow trees. The fairies lived in the ground around these willow trees on the other side of the lake.

Seeing the goal invigorated all three of the sprites, and they practically ran to the other side of the lake. Their hunger, fear, and exhaustion were completely forgotten. As they approached the trees, Edie, Michael, and Abbie could see the fairies flying through the trees. Edie couldn't wait to get to meet the wonderful fairies whom she had always heard about and who would hopefully be able to help her.

As they approached the edge of the lake, the ground became more loose and slippery from the mud, rocks, and tall weeds that accompanied the area. Edie suddenly lost her footing and tumbled to the ground. When she landed, she hit her head on a rock, rendering herself unconscious. The last thing she heard before she was enveloped in darkness was Abbie's terrified scream.

Chapter Four

A Visit with the Fairies

The first thing that Edie heard when she woke up was whispering. She was lying face down on what felt like some sort of cot. Her mouth felt dry, and she lay there on her stomach for a moment, trying to remember what had happened. Edie pushed herself up onto her elbows, frightening the three fairies that were sitting at a table beside her. She blinked her eyes a few times to try to comprehend what was happening. Was she still dreaming? How had she become the same size as fairies? And, where was she?

Edie had never seen the room that she was in. She quickly looked around to see if she could find a clue as to where she was. The whole room looked like it had been carved out of earth. The walls were a tan color and were slightly rounded so that you couldn't tell exactly where the walls ended, and the ceiling began. A glass jar with a firefly in it hung from the center of the ceiling and shed light over the room. Edie's bed frame and the table that the fairies were sitting around were made of wood. Edie didn't know exactly what the bedding was made of, but it was made of the softest material she had ever felt. Her head began to pound, so she quickly lay down on her back. Edie felt a searing pain in her back as it touched the bed, and she cried out in pain. She quickly rolled back over onto her stomach. The pain was blinding, but the sheets felt so soft on her face and arms.

"She's awake!" squeaked one of the fairies. "I've got to go tell her." She scampered out of the room.

Edie wondered whom this "her" could be and why her back hurt so badly. Where was she? Had she been captured and tortured? She lay there with apprehension gripping her heart and hundreds of questions and thoughts swirling through her brain. She tried to get a handle on the escalating panic that she felt. In just a moment, Edie heard the familiar sound of Abbie's voice.

"Edie?" Abbie asked anxiously. "Are you awake?"

"Abbie!" Edie exclaimed as a wave of relief swept through her. She rolled onto her side so that she could see Abbie, catching herself before she rolled onto her back. "What's going on here?"

"How much do you remember, Edie?" Abbie asked her, touching her shoulder lightly.

Edie paused and thought for a moment. Memories of their trip from the Ashcroft Forest were beginning to come back to her. Edie remembered slowly turning into a fox. She remembered why she had come to see the fairies with Michael and Abbie. Her memory stopped short, however, just as they were approaching Holli Lake.

"The last thing I remember is slipping in the mud at the edge of the lake. I remember hitting my head on the rock at the edge of the lake," Edie answered. She hands moved up to her head both to check for a bruise or cut and to see if she still had fox ears. Her hands did not find either of the things she was searching for.

"Wow, you missed all the fun stuff!" one of the fairies exclaimed.

At this remark, Edie and Abbie both looked over at the fairies. Abbie seemed to remember suddenly that the fairies were in the room with them. She looked back at Edie and realized that Edie hadn't met any of the fairies yet.

"Oh, before I tell you what happened, Edie, I guess I should introduce you to the fairies that have been looking after you. This is Becky, Annie, and Jordi," explained Abbie as she pointed to each of them. "Michael and I have been sitting with you, but these three fairies have been making sure that you got better."

Edie looked at the three fairies. Fairies and sprites were not very different. The main thing that separated the two species was height. The only other thing that was different was the fact that sprite wings could be any color of the rainbow, while fairy wings were always white unless the fairy was sick. Their skin colors could vary, as could their eye and hair color. Fairies even dressed similarly to sprites, but their clothes were looser and more flowing.

The three fairies in front of Edie were all rather young mirthful fairies. The one named Becky had short wavy brown hair and brown eyes. Becky was dressed in a long sleeved dark green dress that came down to her ankles. The dress had a rounded neckline in the front and then scooped down in the back to allow for her wings. The dress had a layered skirt that looked like it was blowing in the wind when she walked.

Annie had short brownish-blonde hair and brown eyes. She was wearing a loose light blue top held up with two thin straps. She had a light brown wrap skirt that came halfway between her knees and her ankles.

The third fairy, Jordi, had long straight blonde hair with bangs and constantly brushed her whispy bangs out of her hazel eyes. Jordi wore a dark green skirt that had a shorter outer layer that laced up the sides, and a longer second layer made of lighter fabric that came down to her knees. The loose white shirt she wore had laced up the back around her wings.

They all started talking to her at once. All three of them chattered on for a moment about how happy they were that she was awake and that they had been so worried about her. Edie's head began to pound, and she gave Abbie a look that pleaded with her to get them to leave. Abbie got the meaning of the look and asked the fairies to leave for a few minutes while she talked to Edie alone. They agreed and left quietly.

"Thanks Abbie," sighed Edie, the sudden quiet almost as loud as the three fairies chattering. She tried to sit up so that she could talk to Abbie and winced in pain. Abbie helped her lay back down and sat on the floor so that Edie could see her more easily.

"Where's Michael?" Edie asked.

"Michael's asleep right now. We've both tried to sit here with you all the time. We wanted to try to make sure that one of the two of us was here with you. This morning I was on my way over from breakfast when Jordi came to get me. I'm sorry I wasn't here when you woke up," Abbie replied.

"Aw, I appreciate you both so much," said Edie. "So, what happened after I blacked out?"

"Well, Michael and I carried you the rest of the way around the lake. A fairy guard flew out to ask us what our business was with the fairies. We told him who we were and that we requested permission to speak with the queen. The guard asked us to remain where we were while he checked to see if Queen Sharon would grant us an audience. He returned a few minutes later with the queen. We explained to Queen Sharon what had happened to you. She immediately recognized that your ailments had been caused by a fairy curse, and she agreed to aid your recovery.

Queen Sharon told us that one of their fairies had gone missing, and she figured that the missing fairy was the one who had put the curse on you.

"Queen Sharon accepted the presents that we had brought and called for some fairies to bring us a potion to shrink us to their size. The fairies figured it would be easier to take care of you if you were their size. It would have been very awkward for fairies the size of sparrows to take care of you if you were still six foot tall. They were able to get you to swallow the potion despite you being unconscious.

"Once we had shrunk to their size, the fairies brought us down here underground where they live. They put you in one of their healing rooms. Michael and I were given separate rooms in another living section. Annie, Becky, and Jordi got you settled and then your nurse, Jem, came in to start treating you immediately."

Abbie stopped as she noticed Edie beginning to get emotional. "Will I ever be back to normal, Abbie?" Edie asked finally, timidly.

"They're reversing the effects of the curse right now. The fox tail you had is gone now. Your wings have almost grown back. We were really worried about you the last two days because Jem told us how hard it would be for your body to regenerate your wings. Nevertheless, the fairies have done a very good job taking care of you, so you've healed very well. The only lasting effect of the curse is that your hair is probably going to stay this copper color. You should be back to normal as soon as your wings heal," said Abbie.

Edie sighed and let her body go limp with relief. She felt the soft, moss filled pillow against her cheek. Having her wings grown back certainly explained why Edie had felt that searing pain in her back. Edie pulled a lock of her copper-colored hair around between two fingers and examined it. She didn't really mind the new color. Edie realized that if her hair was the worst thing that she'd have to deal with, then she would definitely be all right.

Just then, the door opened. Michael looked into the room, and a big smile spread over his face when he saw that Edie was awake. He walked over to her and gave her a light hug around the top of her shoulders, being careful not to touch the area around her wings.

"The fairies woke me up and told me that you were awake. I didn't believe them at first, but I'm so glad to see that they were telling the truth! Abbie, did you tell her how worried we've been about her?" Michael asked.

"I certainly did. Edie, you really don't know how glad we are that you're awake," Abbie told her.

The three sprites talked for a few more minutes before Jem came in to check on Edie. Jem was a fairy of medium height with long curly red hair and freckles. She had a merry disposition for a nurse. Jem was excited to see that Edie was awake. She suggested that since Edie needed to get her strength back, Michael and Abbie should take her to the dining hall to get something to eat.

Michael and Abbie helped Edie off the bed and then walked slowly with her over to the dining hall. The fairies had dressed Edie in clothing similar to what they wore. It was a loose woven halter top that went over her neck and gave open space for her wings. They had also put a loose wrap skirt around her lower half. Edie was used to something a little thicker, so her arms and legs were chilly. Abbie noticed her shivering and rubbed her arms as they walked.

"I'll ask Jordi to get something for your arms when I see her this afternoon," Abbie told Edie. Edie nodded, trying to keep focused on walking and not on the pain in her body.

The earthen halls were alive with activity. The corridor that the three sprites were walking down seemed to be the main passageway. Smaller halls stretched off from the main one from both sides. Fairies of all sorts flitted back and forth along the halls.

After a few minutes, Michael, Abbie, and Edie reached the dining room. It was a wide room filled with long wooden tables, and down at the far end a small buffet was set up. Michael and Abbie each made a small salad, and Edie got a bowl of broth. The broth was the best Edie had ever tasted. It was light and warmed her insides as it went down.

Edie enjoyed being able to laugh and joke again with Michael and Abbie. Their journey to Holli Lake had been so tense that it was nice to be able to just relax around each other. After they finished eating, Abbie and Michael could tell that Edie was getting tired, so they walked her back to her room.

Over the next few days, Edie slowly improved. Her wings grew back in a few days and even though they were still tender, they looked great. The food at Holli Lake helped Edie gain her health back. Although she thought that all of the food there was superb, she decided that the fairy cupcakes were the best. They were light, fluffy, and wonderfully sweet. Michael and Abbie were with Edie most of each day now that she was awake. Despite the fact that Annie, Becky, and Jordi annoyed Edie with their chattering, they took very good care of her. About a week after Edie had regained consciousness, Jem told Edie that she should be well enough to go home.

Although the three sprites were sad to leave the fairies, they were excited about being able to go home to the Ashcroft Forest. So that night, they packed their things and prepared for their journey home. The next morning, they met with Queen Sharon.

Edie had been a little apprehensive to meet Queen Sharon for the first time. Even though her appearance was formidable, she quickly put Edie at ease with her regal but gracious manner. She had short silver hair that was done up in tufts. She had piercing blue eyes but was shorter than Edie had expected. She wore a pink dress with a skirt that reminded Edie of rose petals.

Abbie, Michael, and Edie expressed their appreciation to her for the gracious hospitality the fairies had displayed. They offered to show Queen Sharon and the rest of the fairies the same hospitality if they were ever in need. Queen Sharon thanked them for their offer. She told them that if their renegade fairy didn't come home soon that they would have to send out a search party, and they might ask for assistance from the sprites at that time. Queen Sharon then supplied them with provisions for the trip home.

Then the three sprites bid goodbye to Queen Sharon, Jem, Becky, Annie, and Jordi; the last three of whom were teary-eyed. After they had walked a few yards away, the sprites drank the fairy potion that would grow them back to their full size. As Edie swallowed the liquid, a tingling sensation spread through her body. She found that the objects around her quickly grew smaller, and she could feel her body stretching in all directions. In a few seconds, Edie was back to her normal height. Michael and Abbie had drunk their potions at the same time, so they were quickly restored to their full heights as well.

All three of the sprites were anxious to go home, so they quickly took flight and began to head back toward the Ashcroft Forest. Their journey home took just over three days. They had no incidents on the way. However, they were slowed down because Edie's wings were still new and sore, and she tired out after long stretches of flying. Edie was so glad that the return journey went more smoothly than the original. She couldn't wait to get back to the Ashcroft Forest and her own house and bed.

Joneé greeted them as they returned to the village. She was incredibly glad to see that they had all returned safely and gave all three of them big hugs. Fen came out and greeted them and told them that he would call a meeting of the village's council so that Michael, Abbie, and Edie could tell them about their journey.

The three travelers went to their separate houses, set down their supplies, and took a nap. After a few hours rest, Joneé came and woke them up in time for the council meeting. The village council consisted of the four wisest residents of the Ashcroft Forest: Steph, Feath, Kirby, and Bebo. Steph, the only female sprite on the council, had powder blue eyes and burgundy wings. She was one of the most trusted sprites in the Ashcroft Forest and therefore served as Fen and Joneé's assistant. The sprite by the name of Feath had a hairless head, green eyes, dark blue wings, and was in charge of instructing and teaching some of the younger sprites like Michael, Abbie, and Edie. Kirby had helped to establish the sprite village in the Ashcroft Forest many years ago. He was a very strong sprite with green eyes, a bald head, and beige colored wings. Bebo, who was in charge of healing and taking care of the animals in the village, had black hair, sea green eyes, and copper wings.

Joneé and Fen presided over the council meeting. Edie, Michael, and Abbie gave a report of their journey to Holli Lake. The council was glad to hear that the fairies had welcomed the three young sprites and that Edie's curse had been lifted. The three young sprites told the council about the renegade fairy and that the fairies from Holli Lake might soon send out a search party. Michael, Edie, and Abbie also told the members of the council that Queen Sharon had asked for the sprites' help if they started a search for the dark fairy. The council said that they would take that into advisement and deal with it if the need arose. Although the three sprites had been nervous about what the council meeting would invite, it turned out to be rather short. Abbie, Michael, and Edie were allowed to go back to their houses. The three of them were so exhausted that they didn't say anything to each other on their walk to their homes, except a quick goodbye before they each went inside to rest.

Edie was so thankful to be in her own home again. Even though she was tired and sore, Edie unpacked the few things that she had brought back with her from her journey. Once she was content from putting everything away, she dragged herself back to her bedroom. Then Edie gladly crawled into her own bed and fell asleep for the next two days.

Chapter Five

Supreme Kelzer

Edie was glad to wake up in her own bed. Even though the fairies had been gracious to Edie, she was still glad to be home. The area around her wings had healed nicely, although they were slightly bruised from the flight back from Holli Lake. The rest that she had gotten the last two days had helped her body recover from the grueling journey.

Edie got dressed quickly so that she could go over to Abbie's house. She felt more herself in her own clothes. She put on an earth colored corset that came up to just below her wings in the back and laced in the front. She then pulled on some sleeves that went up almost to her shoulders. She pulled on some tan trousers that made her glad that the council did not require female sprites to wear skirts and dresses. That was something Abbie enjoyed, but it was not her style. She pulled on some soft boots that came up to her ankles, and she left her house.

Abbie wasn't at home, so she decided to try Michael's house. On her way over to Michael's house, Catey flew over to her. She gave Edie a big hug.

"Edie!" Catey exclaimed. "I'm so glad you're alright. I was so worried about you!"

About that time, the young sprite named Joe flew up beside them. He was much shorter than both Edie and Catey. Joe had short brown hair, brown eyes, and orange wings. He too embraced Edie and told her how much he had missed her.

Edie winced slightly with each hug. She thanked both of them for their concern and asked them if they knew where Michael and Abbie were. They told her that Abbie, Michael, and a bunch of the other sprites had gone out to the field so that Michael could teach them a new game. She asked them why they weren't going to play, and they replied that they had just come back to get Michael's kelzer. Joe and Catey then scampered off to Michael's house to get the disc.

Edie set off toward the field. As she approached, she saw that several sprites were there to learn this game. When Abbie saw

Edie coming, she ran over to give her a hug. Edie winced again but didn't mention it to Abbie.

"You're up!" Abbie exclaimed as they walked down and joined the cluster of sprites. "I'm happy to see you! Michael's going to teach us a game that he used to play when he lived in the Dixon Glade!"

"That sounds like fun!" Edie said.

The two of them reached the huddle of sprites surrounding Michael. Michael stepped out and gave Edie a big hug as she got to where he was. Fen patted her on the shoulder and told her he was glad to see her up and around again. She was glad for the affection, but the pain from her wings was beginning to get to her.

Several other sprites came up to give her a hug, including Lenk, Mac, and Brendon. She waved them off and apologized. Lenk was a young sprite who loved to play sports and who acted as the village doctor. He had short brown hair, grey eyes, teal-green wings, and was almost as tall as Fen. Mac was a young sprite with short black hair, deeply brown skin, and reddish-orange wings who loved to dance. Although Brendon was a sprite who was intimidating to look at, he was one of the most jovial sprites in the Ashcroft Forest. He had dark skin like Mac, brown eyes, short black hair, and grey wings. Brendon and Joneé had been dating for as long as anyone could remember.

Edie was so glad to be back among her fellow sprites. She couldn't wait to learn a new game with them and be able to have some fun. About that time, Catey and Joe returned to the field. Joe held a flat wooden disc about the size of a plate in his hand. Edie assumed that this was the kelzer. Michael got everyone's attention and then began to explain the game.

"Ok," Michael began. "This game is called Supreme Kelzer. We're going to split up into two teams. I'll be the captain of one team, and I'll get Fen to be the captain of the other team. Yesterday Fen, Lenk, Mac, and I built the goals you see up there."

The group followed his gaze to the top of the trees. Perched in the top of a tree at one end of the field was a goal made out of tree branches. It looked like a five-foot tall cage that was missing the side facing them. There was another goal that matched it on the opposite side of the field.

Michael continued, "The object of the game is to get the kelzer into the goal that's being guarded by a member of the opposing team. Your team gets one point each time your team scores a goal. The first team to get ten points wins. There are a few minor things to go over. The only sprite allowed into the goal at any time is the sprite guarding the goal. If any other sprite enters the goal area, their team loses a point and the kelzer automatically goes to the other team. Also, if it goes behind the goal or into the trees around the field, the kelzer goes to the other team. After your team scores a goal, control of the kelzer goes to the other team. I think that just about covers everything. The game is pretty straightforward, but it's a lot of fun. Do any of you have any questions?"

"I do," Joe piped up.

"Ask away!" Michael replied.

"Since we'll be flying during this game, what happens if someone drops the kelzer, and it hits the ground?" Joe asked.

"Good question, Joe. If it hits the ground, it goes to the opposite team of whoever was in possession of it last," Michael answered. "And there is a time limit on holding the kelzer. You can fly anywhere to throw the kelzer, but don't hold on to it for too long. Try to keep it moving. Does anybody else have any questions?"

Nobody else had any questions. Edie joined Michael's team, along with Abbie, Mac, Walt, and Brendon. Joe, Catey, Feath, Bebo, and Lenk joined Fen's team. Michael made Edie their goalie so that she wouldn't have to fly quite so much. Fen chose Joe to be goalie for their team.

Fen decided to let Michael have control of the kelzer first. Michael threw the kelzer to Mac. Mac deftly avoided Catey and threw the wooden disc to Abbie. Abbie swooped down to catch it, but Fen followed her and blocked her throw to Walt. With Fen's team now in possession of the kelzer, Fen threw the kelzer to Lenk, who darted out from behind Brendon to catch the disc. Brendon however, flew back in front of Lenk and blocked his shot to Catey. Brendon tried to throw the kelzer to Abbie, but Fen again blocked his throw. Fen tried to hold on to the wooden disc, but it slipped from his grasp. Fen and Abbie dove after it, but both were too late, and it hit the ground.

Since Fen had been the last one to touch the kelzer, the disc went to Abbie. Abbie threw the kelzer to Michael. Michael turned and, on a chance throw, managed to get the kelzer past Joe into the goal nearly thirty yards away. As Michael's team cheered and congratulated him, Fen's face hardened slightly. To him, the game had just gotten serious.

Joe gave the kelzer to Feath. Feath darted around Mac and threw the kelzer to Bebo. Bebo threw the kelzer over Michael's head to Fen. Fen made a wild throw toward Catey, but the kelzer sailed into the trees. It landed on top of the goal that Joe was guarding. Fen flew up to get it. He landed on top of the goal.

Fen walked carefully down the criss-crossing wooden supports of the goal. As he bent down to pick up the kelzer, his foot slipped off the wooden beam, and his foot got caught between two beams. Fen struggled to pull his foot free, but he could feel the wooden supports cracking beneath him from his weight. He tried to extricate himself by gaining lift, but he knew he was only wasting his energy. The wood was splintering from the force he was exerting on it. Fen called for help. He heard Feath land on the goal just before the top gave way.

By the time the top gave way, the other sprites had reached Fen. Edie watched in horror as the top broke with Fen still struggling to get his foot free. Fen and the top section of the goal crashed through the bottom of the goal. The force of the impact knocked Fen unconscious, and his body hung limp as he and the broken remnants of the cage hurtled down to the forest floor below.

The sprites quickly descended to see what they could do. The male sprites began moving the debris off Fen. As soon as the Fen was clear of debris, Lenk began checking him to see how badly the fall had injured him.

Lenk began talking aloud as he examined Fen, "His heart's still beating, so he's still alive. He landed flat on his back, which is good because his wings took most of the brunt instead of his internal organs. However, his wings are seriously injured, and it's going to take a long time for them to heal completely. Fen's arms and legs are badly cut and badly bruised in several places. From the look of his right leg, I think it's broken, but we can easily set that and fix it. His right shoulder is either broken or popped out of the socket."

At that point, Lenk gently felt the area around Fen's right shoulder. He called Mac over and asked Mac to hold Fen still. Edie turned away, but she still heard the sickening thud as Lenk pushed Fen's shoulder back into place.

Lenk continued, "That was easily fixed! I'm glad the arm was just out of the socket. It could have been much worse. It looks as though Fen's right side didn't take as much of the brunt on the fall. His right arm and leg look all right even though they're a bit cut and bruised."

He paused for a split second before making his decision. "Alright. We need to move him back to the village, but we need a few things. We've got to have something to minimize the bleeding from his cuts, something to splint his leg with, and something to carry him flat on."

Abbie, Catey, and Brendon volunteered to fly to Lenk's hut to get a stretcher and some things to bandage Fen up. The three sprites quickly returned, and Lenk, Catey, and Abbie prepared Fen for transport. The male sprites carefully lifted Fen onto the stretcher. Then the party solemnly carried Fen to the healing room that connected to Lenk's hut. They laid him face down on one of the healing beds. Fen would have to remain lying on his face through much of his recovery so that his wings would be allowed the best opportunity to heal.

Bebo and Feath left after getting Fen settled so that they could find Steph, Kirby, and Joneé to discuss what they should do. The sprites needed to find someone to lead in Fen's place until he got better.

Edie, Michael, and Abbie stayed for a while to help Lenk. Edie did her best to overcome the squeamish feeling she had at all of these injuries. They got Fen settled, cleaned his cuts, and set his leg and his wings. There wasn't much else any of them could do after that. They left Lenk's hut, but told him that if he needed anything, to let one of them know. The three of them walked in silence to Michael's house. They sat down exhaustedly around Michael's table. After a few minutes, Michael broke the silence.

"Do either of you want something to eat?" he asked.

"I'm not really that hungry, but I guess we should," Abbie replied. "I'll find something for us to eat."

Abbie wandered into Michael's kitchen and began to distractedly make three sandwiches. Edie and Michael didn't speak until she returned. The three of them munched along, each deep in thought. When they had finished their meal, Michael again broke the silence.

"What do you think the council will do?" he asked in a whisper.

"They'll have to find someone to lead the tribe for Fen until he gets better. Joneé could handle all the responsibilities, but it's a lot to ask of her, even for a short time," Abbie answered.

"Abbie is correct. I just don't know whom they'll choose. I guess we'll find out at the meeting they'll have to call tonight," Edie added.

"I know this isn't my fault, but I feel somewhat responsible," Michael said sadly.

"Don't feel guilty, Michael. Accidents happen. You can't shoulder the responsibility for this," Abbie said comfortingly.

Michael nodded. They sat and talked until they heard a knock on the door. It was Bebo letting them know that the council had called a meeting. Edie, Michael, and Abbie followed Bebo to the meetinghouse. Bebo took his seat at the front of the room with Steph, Feath, Kirby, and Joneé. All of the sprites on the dais looked somber. Abbie, Michael, and Edie found Joe, Catey, Walt, Brendon, and Mac and sat with them. All of them looked as serious as Edie felt. Mac told them that Lenk was staying with Fen while the meeting was going on. The rest of the sprites buzzed with curiosity, wondering why this meeting had been called.

Kirby began, "Thank you all for coming on such short notice. I know you're all wondering why we called you here, so we'll make this as direct and brief as we can. Fen had an accident in the woods today."

At this, the whole room gasped and panicked whispers spread through the room. The noise in the room doubled. Kirby motioned for quiet. The roar died down a bit, but there were still scattered whispers in the room.

Kirby continued, "There is no need to panic. Fen is still alive, but he is unconscious and has some severe wounds that are going to take a while to heal. The council and I have decided that we need someone temporarily to step in to take his place and to help

Joneé. After a brief discussion we have decided on the best sprite for this task."

There was a complete silence in the room. Everyone's attention was on Kirby. No one wanted to miss the name of the sprite the council had appointed. Even the whispers died away.

"The sprite that we would like to ask to take on this responsibility is Mac. Mac, would you come up here, please?" Kirby asked.

Mac's jaw dropped. He walked to the front of the room as if in a daze. The sprites applauded him as he moved to the front of the room.

Bebo quieted the crowd. "Please try to make it easy on Mac while he's in this position. He has a lot of responsibility, so let's try to work together through this. One last thing before we adjourn the meeting. I know that all of us are worried about Fen, but he's very sick right now. Therefore, Lenk has asked that Fen have no visitors for the time being. We will let you know when he is allowed to have visitors. Council adjourns the meeting," Bebo finished.

The council took a dazed Mac to the side and talked to him. Edie felt bad for him having to take on all of this so suddenly. She had confidence in him though. She knew that Mac could handle anything.

Although Bebo had said that Lenk didn't want any visitors, Michael, Abbie, and Edie stopped by his hut to see if they could help him with anything. Lenk looked lonely when they walked in, so they stayed to talk with him and tell him what happened. Mac joined them after he had finished talking with the council. He still looked slightly shocked about all that had happened. After a few minutes, he asked the question that everyone seemed to want to know.

"So Lenk, how long is it going to take Fen to recover?" Mac asked seriously.

"Well, let's start with the easiest first. He should be able to walk without crutches in about two months. His leg should be fully healed in six months. His wings will take longer, of course. It'll be about three months before I would let him get up with those wings. They're wrapped up in the proper position so that they will heal correctly without the chance of being moved, but the strain of getting up might re-injure them. It'll definitely be at least seven months before I would allow Fen to even attempt a short flight," Lenk replied.

"And how long before he regains consciousness?" Mac inquired.

Lenk sighed. "I knew you would ask that," Lenk replied quietly. "There's no way to really know when he'll regain consciousness. If he had just hit his head on the top of the goal, he would probably be awake by now. But with the fall that he took, there's no way to know when and if he'll wake up."

Mac, Michael, Abbie, and Edie all gasped. This wasn't a possibility that had yet occurred to them. Fen might never wake up? It seemed too outrageous to be true. The serious look on Lenk's face confirmed it for them though. This realization hit Mac the hardest. He looked straight at Lenk, his face crumbling.

"So, you mean there's a possibility that Fen might never wake up?" Mac asked in a wavering voice.

"Yes. I'm afraid there is that possibility," Lenk sadly answered.

Chapter Six

The Celebration

Mac's blank look spoke for itself. Edie knew that although on the outside Mac was calm, on the inside, his mind was racing from the news. Edie herself was shocked. Her whole body felt numb. The thought that Fen might not survive his fall hadn't even occurred to her. She looked at Michael and Abbie to see how they were reacting. Abbie had begun to cry silently, and Michael looked like he was going to be sick.

The inevitable rush of emotion finally hit Mac. All the stress that Mac had came rushing out in a flood of tears. Abbie and Edie laid their hands on Mac's shoulders to try to give him some sort of comfort. A silence fell over the room so that the only sound any of them heard was the sound of Abbie's sniffles and Mac's sobs.

Mac's tears stopped as abruptly as they had started. He sat slightly hunched over for a few minutes, his head still in his hands. Then Mac raised his head and looked around at the four other sprites in the room. His face was wet, but he was no longer crying.

"Do you think I can do this?" Mac asked, his voice trembling from the emotional flow he had just had.

"Absolutely," Michael replied. "I have complete faith in you."

"I have no doubt," Edie agreed.

"Nor do I," said Lenk.

"Nor I," concluded Abbie.

Mac sat there for a minute. He seemed to wrestle with whether he would accept this or not. Finally, he nodded his head as if in concession.

"Alright. I'll do it," Mac said.

"We all know you'll do a great job. The council wouldn't have selected you if they didn't think that you could fill in for Fen," Abbie encouraged.

"Anyway Mac, you're not doing this by yourself. You're partnering with Joneé, and you know that we'll be here for anything you need," Edie added.

"Of course," said the others, nodding their assent.

"You don't know how much I appreciate all of your support in this. I think I'll be able to take this role until Fen gets better. I have faith that Lenk can help him get well," Mac said optimistically.

"I'm going to do the best I can," said Lenk.

"Good," Mac replied.

"I just remembered something," Lenk said quite suddenly.

"What?" Michael asked.

"Tomorrow is the eighth of the month. The celebration is tomorrow night," Lenk answered.

"Wow. I had totally forgotten about it," Abbie sighed.

"I'll have a busy day tomorrow making sure that everything is in place for it and trying to keep spirits up," Mac said looking tired from the mere thought of it.

"I'm sure things will go fine tomorrow night," Edie said. She laughed. "There's nothing that can compare to that one celebration we had last year. Everyone totally forgot that it was the eighth of the month until about lunchtime that day. It was so crazy trying to throw everything together at the last minute."

Abbie, Lenk, Edie, and Mac all laughed at the memory. They started sharing more stories about things that had happened to them over the years. Michael even shared a few stories about his life in the Dixon Glade. The five of them talked long into the night. When Edie, Michael, Abbie, and Mac headed to their houses, they all felt a bit more positive.

The next day dawned, and the Ashcroft Forest was alive with preparations for that night's celebration. When Michael, Abbie, and Edie saw Mac just before lunch, he said that everything was falling into place and that all of the preparations were running smoothly. Edie, Michael, and Abbie had lunch together and then split up to get ready for the celebration. Abbie went back to her house to put the finishing touches on the new song she had written for the night. She got dressed in a long sleeved flowing white dress and braided her hair into a crown around the back of her head. Michael went out to the field to help some of the male sprites set up the tables and benches. Edie helped carry the food down to the field where they were holding the celebration. In just a few hours, everything was ready, and all of the sprites had gathered.

Mac officially began the festivities. Everyone got their food and sat down to talk with their friends. There was plenty for everyone to share. The celebration seemed to lighten everyone's mood and take their minds off Fen's predicament. Everything went well that night, and the festivities lasted until late into the night.

Michael, Abbie, and Edie stayed to help Mac and Joneé clean up after the celebration had ended. They congratulated Mac and Joneé on doing a great job of pulling everyone together.

"I'm glad things came off so well. It wasn't really any of my doing. Everyone pitched in and helped. I'm so happy that everyone had a good time," Mac said contentedly.

The sprites finished cleaning up and then walked back to their houses. They were all tired, but glad that things had come off as well as they had. Abbie noticed that Michael was rubbing his shoulder and asked if he had injured it or something.

Michael replied, "No. I think that a bee stung me. I was just checking to see if my arm was swollen or something."

"I think I got stung by a bee too," Joneé said. "I felt something poke my elbow while I was eating some of the strawberry tart."

"It probably was just a bee. Bees are all over the place right now. We kind of invaded their territory tonight too, by taking over the field with all those flowers blooming," Abbie replied.

By this time, the sprites had reached the center of the village. The five sprites went to their separate homes and were soon asleep.

Edie woke up the next morning and decided to find a quiet place outside to sketch. Her plans quickly changed however, after she stepped outside her door. The village looked like it had been through a war zone. There was half-eaten fruit everywhere. Joneé's flower garden had been trampled and the blooms from the flowers were gone. There were hoof and paw prints all over the paths.

Edie hurriedly walked to Abbie's house to check and see if she was OK. As Edie walked next door, she saw even more damage. The door to Lenk's house was hanging off its hinges. Abbie's door had scratch marks on it. Edie frantically knocked on Abbie's door.

"Abbie!" she yelled. "Are you OK?"

"What is it Edie?" Abbie asked groggily as she opened the door. Her eyes widened as she looked out the door at the village behind Edie.

"What happened?" she asked.

"I don't know!" Edie exclaimed. "I got up this morning to go find a peaceful place to draw, but I saw all this. I don't know what happened. What should we do, Abbie?"

Abbie contemplated a moment and then replied, "We have to get Mac and Joneé."

Abbie pulled on some slippers and followed Edie out the door. As she closed it, she gasped at the long scratches in the wood. "Well now I know why you were so eager for me to open the door," she told her friend.

Edie nodded silently, and Abbie gave her a quick hug.

Edie and Abbie first walked over to Mac's house. He was horrified when he saw the damage. He joined them as they walked over to Joneé's house. As they approached the front door, Abbie noticed a trail of flower petals that ended at Joneé's front door that was not closed all the way. She pointed it out to Edie and Mac. They both thought it was strange, but Mac went ahead and knocked on the door. It took her a few minutes, but when Joneé finally answered the door, she had two flower petals stuck in her hair. Mac, Edie, and Abbie stared at her for a moment in stunned silence. Abbie was the first to find her voice.

"Joneé," she began. "We woke up this morning to find this mess."

Abbie stopped and gestured behind her. Joneé's mouth dropped open as she looked past the three sprites on her stoop to the debris around the forest. She shook her head and pursed her lips as she surveyed the damage. One of the petals fell out of her hair as she shook her head, startling her. She stared at it on the ground.

"Let's make sure everyone's alright. Then we'll call a town meeting to see if anyone knows what's going on," Joneé said stepping out of the house and closing the door.

Edie grabbed Abbie and Mac by the elbow as Joneé walked on ahead of them.

"Did you see the flower petals in her hair?" Edie asked.

"Yeah," both Abbie and Mac answered.

"Do you remember Joneé and Michael complaining about having been stung by a bee last night?"

"Yes. Why?" Mac asked.

"If you remember a few months back, I was out in the field the night before I began to turn into a fox. I heard something behind me and then I felt something like a bee sting. The next morning Catey found the half-eaten apples around her trees. Do you think there's even the slightest possibility that the renegade fairy that's still on the loose might have turned Michael and Joneé into foxes?" Edie asked worriedly.

Mac shook his head and backed away. "No. This isn't happening. Joneé has to be here to help me run things until Fen gets well. I can't afford to send her to Holli Lake!" Mac exclaimed, still shaking his head.

"As much as I hate to say it, Edie's conclusion does sound plausible. Let's help Joneé check on everyone before she gets suspicious of our conversation. We'll bring it up at the meeting in a bit. Just don't panic for now, Mac," Abbie said.

The four of them walked around the village and checked on the rest of the sprites. All of the sprites were surprised to see the wreckage outside their doors. Although none of them knew how it had happened, some of the houses had debris right up to their doorstep. Joneé told each of the sprites about the meeting she had decided to call right after lunch.

The only house of interest was Lenk's house. The front door was hanging off its hinges, and there were huge scratch marks on the outside. Not knowing exactly how to knock, Mac instead called for Lenk. Lenk walked to the door and looked at it strangely as he pushed it open. It creaked slightly and then fell off completely. They all looked at it for a moment and then looked at each other. Lenk invited Abbie, Mac, Edie, and Joneé in. While Joneé and Mac were asking him the same questions they had asked all the other sprites that morning, Edie looked around Lenk's house. Her eyes stopped on the door that led into the healing room. The door had long scratch marks on it. Edie elbowed Abbie and inclined her head toward the door. Abbie studied the door for a moment and then nudged Mac. Mac looked at the door and then turned to Lenk.

"What happened to the door?" Mac asked.

Lenk looked at the door with a puzzled expression. "I don't know," he replied slowly.

"Lenk. You're honestly going to tell me that something scratched your outside door and basically knocked it off the hinges, then came inside and scratched the door into Fen's room, and you didn't hear anything?" Mac asked incredulously.

"Mac, I don't know what to tell you," Lenk said shaking his head. "I honestly didn't hear anything last night. I must have been sleeping really hard."

Mac turned to Edie. "As much as I hate to, Edie, I may have to admit that you're right," he sighed.

Edie and Abbie both nodded sadly.

"Edie's right about what?" Joneé asked.

"I think she's figured out what's going on," Mac replied.

"And what is it?" Joneé asked slightly impatiently.

"We'll tell you at the meeting," Mac replied to Joneé. He then turned to Edie and Abbie. "You two, follow me."

The three of them left a bewildered Lenk and a frustrated Joneé and walked to Mac's house. Abbie and Edie followed Mac to his kitchen. He began to make lunch, and the three sprites talked while they prepared the food.

"So if this fairy has changed at least Lenk, Joneé, and Michael into foxes, or animals, or something, how many more sprites have the same problem?" Mac asked. "We were all in the field last night. How big do you think this problem is?"

"I don't know, Mac. It could just be that only Lenk, Michael, and Joneé have been affected by this. On the other hand, it could be that there are more. I just don't know. Whatever they're turning into must be pretty big to make long scratches like those on Lenk's doors. I don't think a fox the size that Edie was could have done that kind of damage," Abbie replied.

"This could be a very bad situation," Mac sighed. "But for now, let's just take a minute and enjoy this lunch."

Abbie, Mac, and Edie gathered around Mac's kitchen table and had a quiet lunch. When they were done, the three of them headed over to the meetinghouse. After a few minutes, the whole tribe of sprites that lived in the Ashcroft Forest had assembled.

Mac began the meeting. "I have a question for all of you. How many of you got stung by a bee last night?" he asked.

Hands went up all over the room. Edie looked around the room. The only sprites who weren't raising their hands were Abbie, Mac, Walt, Kirby, Brendon, and Edie herself.

Mac's jaw dropped in horror. His mind began to race. How would all of these sprites be able to go to Holli Lake? How would he be able to keep watch over them on the journey? How would he be able to keep a watch on them until they were able to go? Were they all turning into foxes? If not, what were they turning into? What was he going to do?

Chapter Seven

The Plan

Mac stood there trying to figure out what to do. A murmur of curiosity swept through the crowd. Why would Mac be so concerned about a bee problem? Edie could see the look of panic growing in Mac's eyes. To prevent widespread panic through the rest of the sprites, she stepped up to help Mac.

"We think that we may have had an attack from the renegade fairy that turned me into a fox," Edie began. A slightly more panicked murmur went through the sprites. Abbie closed her eyes and leaned back in her seat. Sometimes Edie's forthrightness was refreshing, but this did not seem like the time to be completely honest about everything, causing everyone to panic.

"There's nothing to panic over," she said, causing Abbie to exhale all at once.

"We just need to quarantine everyone tonight so that we can figure out who exactly might be affected," Edie lied. She knew that every one of the sprites who had acknowledged that they had been stung was affected.

The sprites seemed to calm at this. Mac looked at Edie appreciatively. Edie felt poorly about having to lie to everyone. If it could prevent widespread panic until they figured out what to do, however, then it was worth it.

Edie continued, "So we're going to ask Rufus, Wayne, and Walt to help us put locks on all of the houses. This should be the best way to ensure everyone's safety. Mac and Kirby will be patrolling tonight to keep a check on everyone and see who we'll have to keep in quarantine."

Most of the sprites nodded their agreement. Edie hoped it was alright that she had stepped up and taken charge like this. Mac seemed to have recovered now, so Edie returned to her seat and let him continue the meeting.

"Thank you, Edie," Mac said as she took a seat. "As Edie said, there's not a lot to panic over. We're just taking some precautions to make sure that everyone stays safe. As I adjourn the meeting, I would like to ask Kirby, Abbie, Edie, Brendon, Joneé, Wayne,

Walt, and Rufus to stay for a few minutes. The rest of you are free to go. Wayne, Rufus, or Walt will be by sometime today to put the locks on your door."

The eight sprites that Mac had asked to stay made their way to the front of the room. Michael looked at Abbie and Edie with a knowing but nervous look before heading out the door. Among the sprites who stayed were Wayne and Rufus. Wayne and Rufus built all of the buildings in the Ashcroft Forest. Rufus was Abbie's father. He had jet-black hair, deep brown eyes, and lime-green wings. Wayne was the same height as Rufus, but broader in the shoulders. Wayne had silvery hair, light blue eyes, and beautiful golden wings. Wayne was married to Trista, the village horticulturist. Trista grew many varieties of plants in her backyard. Any time any of the sprites needed plants to make a garden, she had the plants on hand in her backyard. All of the sprites in the Ashcroft Forest marveled at the lovely flowers she grew. Trista had glittering pink wings, green eyes, and shoulder length blonde hair.

"Alright," Mac began as the sprites sat around him. "I need to have a serious talk with you."

"Before you go into a long explanation, let's go ahead and cut to the chase. All of us that raised our hands have the same type of curse that Edie had, right?" Wayne asked pointedly. "That's why you looked so upset after we had raised our hands, isn't it?"

Mac looked momentarily shocked and then answered, "Yes, Wayne. I was surprised at the fact that such a large number of sprites had been cursed. We're not quite sure what we're going to do next, but we do have to make sure that we don't end up accidentally killing each other. It appears that Kirby, Walt, Abbie, Edie, Brendon, and I are the only ones that have somehow escaped the curse. I agree with Edie's earlier suggestion, and would like to ask that Rufus, Wayne, and Walt go around and put locks and barricades on all of the doors. If there are two people living in a house, make sure that they are somehow separated and have a locking door between them. Put the lock on the outside of the door so that we can lock them in tonight and then unlock the door in the morning. Will you be willing to help us out with this?"

"We are more than willing to do this, Mac. However, before we go, I have one question for you," Rufus said.

"Sure. Ask me anything," Mac replied.

"If we were foxes or some kind of animal last night, why don't we remember it?" Rufus asked.

"I can answer that for you," Edie replied. "The first few nights that I was a fox, I don't remember anything that happened. The stronger the curse was on me and the more I became a fox, the more I started to remember of my nightly outings, and the more I began to be able to harness what I did each night. Those first few days I don't remember anything of what I did, including eating the apples from Catey's tree." She shook her head at the memory.

"Alright," Rufus accepted. "I understand. Wayne, Walt, and I will get to work putting the locks on and leave you to figure out what to do about the whole situation."

"Thanks Wayne, Rufus, and Walt," Mac said as the three male sprites got up to leave. "When you finish, make sure that Walt has the keys to the locks. Walt, you'll be in charge of making sure that everyone is locked in at night and unlocking the doors in the morning."

The three male sprites nodded and then left. Mac turned back to the few sprites that remained.

"So how do we handle this, Joneé?" he asked.

"You're sure that this is all attributable to the renegade sprite?" Joneé replied with a question.

"It makes sense, Joneé. The destruction of the camp, the bee stings, and the fact that I was down in the field when the fairy attacked me all fit together. I'm fairly certain that the fairy is the culprit. Tonight will reveal the truth though," Edie said.

"Alright," Joneé agreed. "I trust your judgment. What we need to do then is to have two of the sprites that were not cursed go to the fairies and beg them to come here to the Ashcroft Forest to return us to our normal state. If I remember correctly, Queen Sharon also promised to catch the misguided fairy that put a curse on us. So, they should be able to come out here and heal us while they look for the missing fairy. Would any of you be willing to go to Holli Lake?"

"I'll go," volunteered Edie.

"I'll go with her," Abbie also volunteered.

Joneé nodded her appreciation. "It would probably be best if the two of you went. You both already know the fairies and know how to negotiate with them. Thank you," she said.

Joneé then turned to the four male sprites. "The four of you will be in charge of keeping the peace at night. We've already entrusted Walt with the job of locking all of the doors and unlocking them in the morning. When night falls tonight, make sure to look in the windows and see if all of us have indeed turned into foxes or some kind of animal. Whether we have or we haven't changed into animals, keep us locked in the whole night. During the night, at least two of you need be patrolling at all times. That way we can make sure that if we do indeed turn into animals, we don't escape," she said.

"I just thought of something," said Brendon. "If Lenk has the curse on him, what do we do about Fen? We can't leave Fen in there with a wild animal all night. Doors only do so much. Do you remember the claw marks on Fen's door? I bet they came from Lenk's animal form."

"Good point, Brendon. I'll explain the situation to Lenk and get him to stay in my house at night. Lenk can still look after Fen during the day, and we'll get Walt to stay with Fen at night in case something major happens. I'm sure Lenk will understand," Mac replied.

"Good plan," said Joneé. "I'll leave it to the four of you to sort out how you want to patrol. Abbie and Edie, go get packed to leave tomorrow morning."

The sprites went off to do their separate errands. Mac went to ask Wayne, Rufus, or Walt to secure the locks on his house and to ask if Walt would stay with Fen at night. Then Mac went to talk to Lenk about the two of them switching houses at night. The other two male sprites went to get a bit of sleep before their night watch. Joneé went to make sure the locks on her house were sufficient. Abbie and Edie headed to pack for their trip.

Michael saw Abbie and Edie walk past on their way to their houses. He ran outside and called to them. They turned and saw him coming toward them.

"Come inside with us," Abbie called as she turned back toward her house.

Michael followed Abbie and Edie into Abbie's house. He watched as the two of them began packing some of the food from Abbie's pantry.

"Where are the two of you going?" he asked.

"We've got to go back to see the fairies," Edie replied, still packing.

"Has this got to do with the renegade fairy? Or are you having some kind of relapse?" Michael asked suddenly seeming to doubt himself and the situation.

"I'm fine," Edie said, putting her hand on his arm to reassure him. "You were right to begin with. The fairy has struck again."

"I'm going with you," Michael said determinedly. "I know that since I got stung, I've been cursed as well. I'm going with you to help you. I know it'll be a challenge, but you will need help."

Abbie looked at Edie, who was adding a container of peanut butter to her bag. Abbie looked back to Michael and just shook her head. This time she reached out and took Michael's arm. "You know that wouldn't be the best idea, Michael."

"But I don't want to just stay here..." Michael said quietly. Abbie looked at him and saw the fear in his eyes.

"Michael, you heard Mac. He's got a plan. And he has sprites to help him. You know more about this than the other sprites from being around me, so you will probably be able to control your actions easier than the other sprites," Edie told him matter of factly.

To this, Abbie nodded and then gave Michael a hug. Edie saw the fear disappear from Michael's eyes with that one hug. He seemed resolute that he wouldn't give in to fear.

"We've got to pack quickly. We are going to leave in the morning to go to Holli Lake to ask the fairies to come here," Abbie said turning back to her packing.

"Is there any way I can help?" Michael asked.

"We need all the help we can get to be able to pack quickly," Edie replied.

"Alright then," Michael said helping them put food into a bag.

The sprites got the food packed quickly. The three of them packed a few clothes and things for Abbie. Then they walked over to Edie's house and got clothes for Edie to wear on the journey.

Edie, Michael, and Abbie finished packing late that afternoon. They had a quick dinner and then walked Michael home.

"Wait," said Michael, grabbing Abbie's arm as she turned to leave. "Will I get to see you two in the morning before you leave?"

Abbie glanced at Edie and then back at Michael. "Absolutely," she replied. "We'll wait until they unlock your door before we leave."

"Good," he replied with a relieved smile. "You two be careful tonight."

"We will," Abbie said as Walt arrived to lock Michael in for the night.

"Good night, Michael," Abbie and Edie called before Walt shut and locked the door. Michael stood resolutely at the door before the door closed completely.

Walt locked the door and then turned to Edie and Abbie. "Only a few more houses to lock up," he told them.

Edie and Abbie followed him as he locked up the rest of the houses. The very last house was Joneé's house. She, like Michael warned them to be careful. After promising that they would, the three of them walked to Mac's house. Mac, Kirby, and Brendon were already waiting for them in Mac's living room.

"We made sure that everyone was locked in properly," Walt informed the other sprites. "Now all we have to do is wait until dark and then go check to see if our theory about this is correct."

Chapter Eight

The Quest Begins

When night finally fell, Mac led the group of sprites who had escaped the curse out to check on everyone. It was eerie to be out just after dark and find the whole Ashcroft Forest quiet. Most nights the sprites of the Ashcroft Forest were up late. Edie found the silence a bit frightening. She was glad that Abbie was with her.

Every now and then, the sprites heard strange noises coming from the houses. The first house the six of them walked up to was Bebo's house. At first, they didn't see anything through the window. The light of Kirby's candle just illuminated the blackness inside Bebo's house. Then they saw a huge shape move in the darkness. The huge brown shape came complete with a set of antlers. A large caribou's snout appeared in the window. Bebo the caribou stared into the faces of six surprised sprites.

The sprites hurried from the window. When they were a short distance away, Mac turned to the others. "Well, our suspicions were correct. Good deduction, Edie," he said patting her on the back. Now we know that the other sprites are able to turn into animals besides foxes. Let's see how the other sprites are faring. This should be interesting."

The other sprites nodded and followed him. They heard scratching and howling as they approached Michael's house. Edie cautiously peered in the window. She and the other sprites, who walked up behind her, saw Michael the wolf was pawing frantically at the bottom of the front door to try to get out. Abbie felt bad for having to keep him locked up, but she knew it was best for all of them.

Brendon led them over to Joneé's house next. He was glad to see that she had taken the shape of a gentle doe. Brendon also realized that Joneé had ironically been the one who had eaten the purple flowers she was so proud of.

Edie and Abbie walked up to Trista and Wayne's house. When they peered into the windows, they were glad that the two of them had been locked into two different areas of the house. The two of them actually wondered how Trista had survived the first night under the curse with Wayne. Wayne had been turned into a huge grizzly bear, and Trista had been turned into a small brown rabbit.

Brendon, Kirby, Mac, Walt, Abbie, and Edie continued to walk among the houses to check on the cursed sprites. Catey had been turned into a porcupine. Joe the chipmunk was trying to find a way to get out through the window. Steph had been transformed into a raccoon and was rummaging through her cabinet. Feath was now a bald eagle. He was perched on a chair in his living room looking for a means of escape. Rufus had taken on the shape of an owl. Although the sprites approached his house quietly, he turned and looked directly at them as they reached his window. It was an eerie feeling.

The scariest situation they came upon was Lenk. The sprites were incredibly relieved that Lenk and Mac had switched houses for the night. Lenk had become a cougar. Lenk the cougar was scratching Mac's door desperately to try to get out. It was ironic that one of the gentlest sprites in the Ashcroft Forest had been turned into such a dangerous animal. After they had checked on all of the cursed sprites, the sprites gathered outside of Mac's house.

"It looks like we'll be running a zoo for the next few days," Mac said with a laugh. The other sprites laughed as well. It was nice to have a bit of levity in such a bad situation. "Seriously though, we did the right thing. I'm glad you recognized what was going on, Edie."

"I'm glad I could help," Edie replied.

Mac turned to the three male sprites. "I've split the four male sprites into two shifts so that we can keep an eye on everyone. Abbie and Edie will be going home to get some rest before they begin their journey in the morning. Walt, you'll be staying in Lenk's house and making sure that nothing happens to Fen for the first half of the night. Then I will take over the second half of the night. Kirby and I will take the first shift and then Brendon and Walt can take the second shift. While we're not actively on patrol at night, we need to sleep because we'll still have to be awake to do our normal duties during the day. Abbie and Edie, I'll see the two of you in the morning."

Brendon, Walt, Abbie, and Edie bid Kirby and Mac goodnight. The four of them walked to their houses. Edie was about to walk into her house when Abbie stopped her.

"Edie?" Abbie asked.

"Yes," Edie replied.

"Do you think we'll be able to make it to the fairies and back in time to save everyone?" Abbie asked.

"I hope so," Edie replied as chipperly as she could. "After all, this is only the second night. It took almost a week after I had been turned into a fox before we left to go to Holli Lake. The more I became like a fox, the slower we got. We won't have an obstacle like that this time, so we should make better time."

Abbie nodded. "So don't worry about it, Abbie. We'll make it in time," Edie said convincingly.

Abbie gave Edie a hug, and the two of them headed into their separate houses. Abbie slept restlessly that night. The next morning dawned much too soon for Abbie's taste. She got up, however, and met Edie in the front yard.

A tired-looking Walt was walking around and unlocking houses. Michael's door had already been unlocked, and he was walking over to say goodbye to Edie and Abbie. Michael waved as he saw the two sprites headed toward him.

"How did it go last night?" Michael asked as he reached them.

"It went pretty well as far as we know," Abbie answered. "We walked around and checked on everyone last night and then went to bed. I'm sure that Kirby, Walt, Mac, and Brendon had everything under control. We checked on you before we went to bed. You turned into a wolf."

Michael's eyebrows rose slightly. "Really?" he asked.

"Yes," Abbie replied.

"Wow. That's really cool and really scary all at the same time," he said.

The two female sprites nodded distractedly. "Well, I know you've got to go now, but I'm so glad I got to see you. I wish I could go with you, but..." Michael trailed off.

"Don't worry about us, Michael," Edie replied. "We'll look after each other. Your job is to stay here and help out during the day and to do your best to control your actions at night."

The two of them hugged Michael. Then they turned to go. Just like the night before, Michael caught Abbie's arm as she started to walk away. She turned back and looked at him.

"Be careful, Abbie," Michael said looking at her with concern.

"Don't worry. I will be," she promised.

Abbie gave him another quick hug and then scampered after Edie who had continued walking. The two sprites walked over to Lenk's house and told Mac goodbye. Rufus met them at Lenk's house to tell them goodbye as well. They admonished them to be careful, and then Abbie and Edie set off for Holli Lake.

The weather was good for flying that day. Although Edie was concerned about the sprites in the Ashcroft Forest, she was glad that she wouldn't have to worry as much on this trip to Holli Lake. Edie looked over at Abbie. Abbie looked lost in thought about something. Edie knew Abbie must be tired, so she decided to ask her about it later.

About noon, Abbie saw a dark cloud form on the horizon. She nudged Edie and pointed it out to her. At the rate they were flying, it wouldn't take long before the two of them reached the cloud. They decided to try to find somewhere to eat lunch while they waited out the storm. Abbie and Edie descended to the forest floor and scouted for shelter.

Edie searched for a few minutes and found the perfect spot. Just a short walk away from where she was standing was a medium sized hill. In the side of the hill was a huge opening that was about ten feet in diameter. Edie found Abbie, and the two of them slipped inside the opening just as it started to rain.

"We just barely made it inside," Abbie said as she unpacked their bread and peanut butter.

"Yes. I'm glad I found this place," said Edie looking at the rain that was now pouring down.

Abbie nodded her agreement as she began to eat. Her eyes seemed to haze over as if she was deep in thought. Edie looked at her for a moment and then decided that now was the time to ask her what she was thinking about.

"Is everything alright, Abbie?" Edie asked her.

Abbie came out of her reverie and looked at Edie blankly for a moment. Her eyes unclouded, and she seemed to snap back to reality.

"What?" Abbie asked alertly.

"Is everything alright, Abbie?" Edie repeated.

"Yes. I'm just worried about whether or not we'll make it in time," she replied.

"Abbie, we already talked about that," Edie said gently. "I thought we both agreed that it shouldn't be a problem."

"I know," Abbie replied with a sigh.

"So what's going on?" Edie asked.

"I'm just worried about Michael. Even though he tried to hide it, I think he's really scared about the curse. And he seemed so concerned for our safety," Abbie said.

"Michael may be a bit scared, but he'll be fine. He knows what happened with me, so he knows a lot of what's going to happen to him. So don't worry about him," Edie replied.

Abbie sighed again as she looked out at the rain. It was starting to fall more slowly now, turning into a light drizzle.

"I know you're right, Edie," Abbie said. "He's just been such a good friend since he's been here, and I hate to leave him alone at a time like this." She paused for a second. "I'm also worried about my dad."

"Michael will be fine and so will Rufus. The other sprites will look after him. It's not as though we're leaving them forever anyway. We'll be home in a few days," Edie said reassuringly.

"Are you sure about that?" a raspy voice behind them asked.

Abbie and Edie looked at each other with fear in their eyes and then they slowly looked behind them. Crouched behind them on the ground was a huge creature with purple scales and blue wings. It had four legs, clawed toes, and a long tail with blue spines on the back.

The dragon looked at them through its fiery red eyes. "So, what have I done to deserve having two such beautiful young sprites delivered to my doorstep?" it asked slyly.

Edie and Abbie both moved toward the mouth of the cave, but the dragon was too quick for them. It moved its tail across the entrance and flicked it back and forth. They were trapped. There was no way they could get out without being crushed by the dragon's moving tail. Edie glanced at Abbie and gulped. She knew they were in a very tough spot.

Chapter Nine

In the Dragon's Lair

Edie's mind began to race. How would they get out of this? Edie had never encountered a dragon herself. She had heard plenty of stories about them though. Most of them were just tales, but a few were actual stories. Dragons loved to eat sprites. They were a delicacy for them because of the sprites' speed and ability to fly. The only way that sprites could escape is either to slay the dragon or to try to hide and then escape.

Edie also knew that dragons were lonely creatures. Dragons were known to enjoy having their prey entertain them before they became dinner. Edie figured she could use that time to work out a plan for their escape. The situation seemed hopeless because they had no weapons, but she figured she could try to come up with something.

Sure enough, the next words out of the dragon's mouth were, "I am Parvack. Tell me about yourselves, my dears. Don't leave anything out. I love stories, and I've got all the time in the world."

He chuckled to himself before adding, "And now, so do you. Or at least, all the time I choose to give you."

The dragon settled in to listen to what Abbie said. Abbie looked at Edie and then began to prattle about the Ashcroft Forest, the other sprites that lived with them, and the renegade fairy that had cursed the other sprites. At mention of the curse, the dragon's face changed from mild amusement to intense interest.

"You say a fairy put this curse upon them?" Parvack interrupted.

"Yes," answered Abbie.

"How do you know for sure? Did you see the fairy?" the dragon asked.

"We didn't see the fairy ourselves, but Edie had this same curse put on her about a month ago. We took a journey to Holli Lake, and the fairies were able to heal her," Abbie answered. "That's where we were headed now."

"Did this fairy do anything else to any of the other sprites that live in your forest?" Parvack inquired.

"No, the only curse to have befallen our sprites is the animal curse. Why?" Abbie replied.

"About two months ago a young fairy entered my cave. I didn't see it, but I could smell it. It must have seen me when it darted in because its smell left quickly. Ever since that day, I haven't been able to leave the bounds of my cave. It was a stroke of good fortune that the two of you happened to stumble into my cave, because I've begun to get hungry," he said licking his lips.

Parvack stopped for a moment and seemed to be deep in thought. "I'm considering something. Be quiet and let me think for a moment," Parvack said turning his head away, but leaving his restless tail at the entrance to the cave.

Abbie and Edie sat together in silence. Edie was still trying to think of a way to escape. The more she thought, however, the more panicked she became at the prospect that there was no way out. Her eyes desperately scanned the cave for anything they could use to kill the dragon, but she could find nothing around. Edie sighed, feeling disappointed in herself. There was also no light filtering in from any other part of the cave, so she knew there was no other opening. She looked over at Abbie. Abbie knew how to keep a calm front. Edie figured that on the inside, however, Abbie was just as scared as she was.

The fear took a lot out of Edie, and she felt herself drifting off to sleep. She woke up with a start at the sound of Parvack's voice. As Edie glanced out the mouth of the cave, she realized that she must have been asleep for hours, because the sky was dark.

"I have reached a conclusion," the dragon began. Abbie and Edie waited nervously to see what this conclusion might be.

"Alright," Parvack said. "Here is the offer I'm willing to make with you. I do not know where Holli Lake is, nor do I think that a group of fairies would be willing to help a dragon. However, I know that since the fairies have already helped you, they would be willing to work with you. I will allow you to go free if you do something for me. I ask that you go to the fairies, ask them to come to the cave, and free me from the curse."

"Absolutely," Abbie and Edie agreed.

The dragon laughed a low rumbling roar of a laugh at their quick agreement.

"Not so fast. Always listen to the whole offer before you accept," Parvack warned.

"My one stipulation is that one of you must stay here as my captive. The other sprite will have four days to get to Holli Lake and back. If the sprite that leaves is not back by dawn on the fifth day, I will eat the one that stayed behind. However, if you make it back in that time, you will both be free to go, and I will owe you one favor," the dragon finished.

Abbie and Edie looked at each other. This looked like the best hope to Edie. She could think of no other way out of this mess. Parvack suddenly spoke again.

"I will give you a moment to discuss this and make a decision," the dragon said.

Parvack turned his head to give them a sense of privacy. Edie knew that dragons had excellent hearing. So even though Parvack's head was turned, he could still hear everything that Abbie and Edie said.

Edie turned to Abbie. "This looks like our only hope, Abbie," Edie whispered quickly.

"I know," Abbie agreed. "Who of us do you think should be the one to go to Holli Lake?"

"I'll go," Edie volunteered. "Since I had this curse before, I think I should go. I hate to leave you like this, Abbie." Her stomach sank at the thought of having to leave Abbie in this predicament.

"No, don't feel bad at all, Edie. I think you're right. I agree that it would be better if you were the one who went to see the fairies. Are you sure your wings will hold out?" Abbie responded.

"They're back to their old strength. I think I'll have plenty of strength to make it to Holli Lake and back."

"Alright then," Abbie agreed.

Parvack turned his head back to face them. "So have you reached a decision about what you'd like to do, my dears?" he asked.

"Yes we have," Edie answered. "Abbie will remain here with you, and I will fly to Holli Lake to get the fairies. I will come back with them and the cure."

"Very well," Parvack replied. "Morning is dawning on your first day. I will give you four whole days. If you are not back with the fairies by dawn on the fifth day, you have no reason to return.

Abbie will not be here, and I will still be hungry. You might want to get going."

Edie grabbed her provisions and quickly hugged Abbie goodbye. Edie hated to leave Abbie in this predicament, but Edie knew that Abbie could take care of herself. Edie took one last look behind her, hoping it would not be the last time she would ever see her best friend, and then set off in the direction of Holli Lake.

Edie would have enjoyed the beauty of that morning's sunrise on any other day, but she was far too worried even to notice it. Edie tried to pace the speed of her flight. She knew she would need her strength for the return flight, but her fear for Abbie accelerated her speed. Edie couldn't bear to think about what would happen should she not be successful with her mission. She flew on, sure of her course.

The sun rose higher and higher in the sky until it was directly overhead. Edie realized that it was noon, and she hadn't had anything to eat since the previous noon. Although she still didn't feel hungry, Edie knew she should eat something to keep up her strength. As she glanced below her for a place to land, she saw a field of wild berries below her. Edie landed in the field and picked and ate as many berries as she thought she could eat. She realized as she was eating that she, Abbie, and Michael had stopped in this very field on their first journey to Holli Lake.

Feeling quite refreshed from the rest and the food, Edie continued on her journey. The rest of the time she spent flying that day was uneventful. In fact, the short time during the night that Edie allowed herself to sleep was uneventful.

Edie awoke the next morning after only a few hours of sleep and set off once again toward Holli Lake. She figured that at the rate she was going, she would reach the fairies just before dusk. Edie hoped that she could explain the situation and get the fairies to leave for Parvack's cave before the dawn of the next day. If everything went according to her plan, and they had no interruption, she should get back in time to rescue Abbie.

Edie pushed thoughts about Abbie out of her mind. The two of them had never been this far apart before. Any time Edie's thoughts began to turn toward Abbie, her fear consumed her almost to the point of literally being frozen in fear. So, Edie instead tried to focus all of her attention on what she had to do.

As the time approached for her to have lunch, Edie realized that she was very near Holli Lake. She ate a lunch of some mushrooms and edible greens. She was glad she had paid attention to Michael's lessons about which mushrooms and greens were edible. Edie ate with enthusiasm, glad that she would reach the fairies sooner than she had expected. When Edie had finished eating, she quickly returned to the air. She wanted to lose no time, especially since she was this close.

About mid-afternoon, Holli Lake appeared on the horizon. In just a few minutes, Edie had arrived at the willow trees on the other side of the lake. Edie waited for a moment for one of the guards to see her. After just a moment, a well-armed fairy flew up to greet her.

"State your name and your business," the guard said.

"I'm Edie from the Ashcroft Forest, and I'm here to talk to Queen Sharon," Edie said.

"Oh, you're the one that had turned into a fox, right?" he asked with a sniff.

"Yes," she replied, surprised that he had remembered her.

"Alright. I'll let Queen Sharon know that you're here," he said flying off.

Edie sat on the grass to wait for the guard to come back. She realized after the guard had left that there were probably few sprites visiting, so that's why he remembered her. She suddenly felt quite tired, but she knew that this was not the time to fall asleep. The hardest part of her quest was about to come. Edie didn't know how difficult it might be to convince Queen Sharon to come with her to Parvack's lair. She hoped that Queen Sharon would be sympathetic to her situation and help her out.

In a few minutes, the guard returned with a bottle that almost dwarfed him and told Edie that Queen Sharon had granted Edie an audience. The guard gave Edie the bottle of shrinking potion to drink. As Edie swallowed the liquid, the world began to grow around her. When she had shrunk to the size of the guard, he escorted her to Queen Sharon's chambers. He took her pack for her and left it outside of the queen's chambers.

"Edie from the Ashcroft Forest, it's good to see you," Queen Sharon greeted her as Edie walked into the room. She rose from her seat, and Edie gave her best attempt at a bow.

"Queen Sharon," Edie replied.

"So what brings you back so soon to Holli Lake?" Queen Sharon asked.

Edie explained the entire situation to Queen Sharon. The queen listened intently as Edie spoke. When Edie finished, Queen Sharon sat back in her chair and studied the wall behind Edie. After a few moments, her eyes returned to Edie.

"Edie," Queen Sharon began, "I, of course, have no problem going and helping the sprites of the Ashcroft Forest. We should have already sent the search party to look for the renegade sprite. This situation would have been prevented had we been proactive in our search. I also see the predicament that your friend Abbie is in, but I just don't know that I can justify sending my fairies into that kind of danger to rescue her. Did Parvack promise safety to us if we went to help him?"

"No," Edie conceded begrudgingly.

Queen Sharon shook her head. "Then I do not believe that I can send my fairies into that kind of danger," she said.

Edie opened her mouth to appeal, but Queen Sharon put up her ringed hand. She continued, "Edie, as I said, Abbie's predicament is regrettable, but I have to consider the safety of my fairies first. I will deeply consider it, but I'm letting you know that the chance of my approval is very slim. Regardless of what I decide, I will prepare a team of fairies to leave for the Ashcroft Forest at dawn tomorrow. We will give you a room for tonight so that you can rest for tomorrow's trip. I will let you know my decision about Parvack in the morning."

Edie's head dropped as she gave her thanks and was ushered out of the room. She knew that the discussion was over. Any argument she tried to make would just make the situation worse. Edie allowed the guard to show her to the room they were providing for her. The room contained just a bed with a small cabinet.

When the guard left, she flopped down on the bed dejectedly. She gave a deep sigh as she sunk into the comfortable bedding. She shook her head, trying to keep herself awake so that she could think. She couldn't give up on Abbie. There had to be a way to rescue her. She needed some time to think.

Chapter Ten

Queen Sharon's Answer

Edie didn't know how long she had been asleep. She hadn't meant to fall asleep in the first place. Edie had been thinking so hard about a plan to rescue Abbie that she had exhausted herself. She had awoken to the noise of tapping. At first, Edie thought it was a bird tapping on her window. Then she realized that she was not, in fact, in the Ashcroft Forest. She was still in the nightmare reality where Abbie was being held captive by a dragon. As Edie sat up, she realized that someone was knocking on the door to her room. Edie opened the door to find the guard standing outside.

"Queen Sharon has requested that you come to her chambers," he said simply.

"Alright," said Edie, still a bit groggy from the sleep. She followed the fairy back down the hall to the room where she had met with Queen Sharon just a few hours before. Edie wondered what Queen Sharon could want with her now. The guard walked to the door, opened it, and allowed Edie to walk into Queen Sharon's chambers.

Edie jumped slightly as the door banged shut behind her. At first glance, the room seemed to be empty. Then Edie saw that Queen Sharon was sitting in a chair at the end of the room. Queen Sharon looked up as Edie entered. She was still wearing the same dress that she had been wearing the last time that Edie saw her, but she did not look disheveled.

"I've reached my decision about whether or not we will help you rescue Abbie," Queen Sharon said as she stood up. Edie braced herself for the bad news. She felt her stomach drop despite her best attempts. She knew that if Queen Sharon refused to help Abbie, then there was little hope for Abbie's survival.

"I've mulled the situation over since you left my chambers earlier," Queen Sharon said. "As you know, at first I was very much against helping you rescue Abbie. This is not because I do not care for her, but only because I must put the good of my fairies first. The more that I thought about it, however, the more I began to wonder what I would do if a friend of mine were in a situation like this. I put myself in your shoes and realized that I had to help you."

"What?" Edie asked in disbelief. Queen Sharon had said it so fast that she thought she had misunderstood.

"We're going to help you," Queen Sharon repeated.

The tightness and fear that had gripped Edie released its hold. She was so relieved. She opened her eyes wider so that she would not cry from relief. Edie wanted to run over and give Queen Sharon a hug, but she decided it would be inappropriate to hug someone of her station. Instead, she looked Queen Sharon in the eye and said as evenly as she could, "Thank you."

"You are welcome," Queen Sharon replied. "I have already assembled a team to go to the Ashcroft Forest. On our way, we will stop by Parvack's lair and rescue Abbie. Time is of the essence. If you are ready to go, we will leave now."

"As soon as I get my things, I'm ready to leave," Edie said turning to the door.

"Your things should be sitting right outside the door," Queen Sharon replied. "I asked my guard to go back and get them after you left."

Edie walked to the door and looked out. Just as Queen Sharon had said, her things were sitting just outside. On the floor beside Edie's knapsack was a wooden box with a leather strap attached to it. Edie gathered both things and turned back to Queen Sharon.

"This isn't mine," said Edie, holding out the box.

"Take it with you anyway. You'll need it," Queen Sharon replied walking to the door. "Follow me."

Edie didn't argue and picked up the box. Queen Sharon led Edie out the door and down a hallway. The two of them walked a bit farther and then they emerged from a small opening that led them outside. A large group of fairies was waiting for Edie and Queen Sharon as they stepped outside. Edie recognized most of them from her previous visit, but she did not remember their names. Then she saw three that she did remember. Annie, Becky, and Jordi ran over and gave Edie a hug. Jem smiled and waved from where she was.

The sun was just peeking through the trees on the opposite side of Holli Lake. Edie was glad that she had only slept until morning. She knew that they would need all of two days to make it back to Parvack's lair.

"Everyone listen to me carefully," Queen Sharon said as the fairies gathered around her. "We are on our way to heal the sprites of the Ashcroft Forest. On our way, we are going to make a slight detour. Edie's friend Abbie, whom some of you may remember, has been captured by the dragon Parvack."

At the mention of the dragon, the fairies collectively gasped. Annie, Becky, and Jordi turned to Edie with worried expressions on their faces, but she kept her attention on Queen Sharon. Queen Sharon continued, "We are going to lift a curse put on Parvack and thereby rescue Abbie. Then we will complete our journey to the forest. If there are any of you who would like to stay behind, now is your time to back out of the journey."

The fairies looked amongst each other, but none of the fairies moved to leave. As Edie looked at those gathered, they all had resolute and determined looks on their faces.

When Queen Sharon had given them time to make their decision, she continued. "Alright. We had a small dilemma about how we would all get to Parvack's lair safely. The best way for us fairies to go, is to remain small. The problem is that if we are to remain small, we won't be able to keep up with Edie. So my counselors and I debated about how we could accomplish this. After much deliberation, we came up with an idea. Edie," Queen Sharon said, turning to face the sprite. "Hold out the box in your hands."

Edie obeyed. As she held out the box, she noticed something on the side that she hadn't seen before. There was a small latched door on one side of it. Edie wondered what the box could be for, but she knew that she would soon find out.

"This is a box made of old magic. A box we have not had to use in many years. It allows anything that is inside it to be transported with ease. The inside of the box is much larger than the outside would reveal. So what we fairies will do is all get inside the box," Queen Sharon told them.

Some of the fairies began to look a bit skeptical at this explanation. Queen Sharon held up her hand for silence.

"Allow me to finish before you reject this idea," she requested. "We will all get into the box. The magic of the box is that no matter how much turbulence we encounter on the trip, we won't feel it. In fact, we won't feel that we've moved at all."

Queen Sharon continued, "Once we're all inside the box, Edie will fly to Parvack's lair. When she stops along the way to rest, she'll knock on the top of the box and then open the door so that we can get some fresh air. Then we will know that it's safe to come out.

"When we get to Parvack's lair, a few of us will go into his lair to lift the curse from him. We'll thereby rescue Abbie and be free to go to the Ashcroft Forest. We are going to be taking enough of the growing potion with us so that once we get to the Ashcroft Forest we can work more easily at sprite height. We will not take the growing potion now, so that we can save our energy for healing the sprites and so that we can stay together more easily.

"So what do you think? Are all of you ready?"

"Of course we are ready!" Jordi cried enthusiastically. She looked around as though she had thought others would join her, and put her hands over her mouth sheepishly. Though some of the fairies still looked skeptically at the box Queen Sharon held, they nodded their agreement.

"Good. Then we'll go ahead and give Edie the growing potion," said Queen Sharon motioning for the guard fairy to come over. The guard walked over and handed Edie a flask containing the potion to make her resume her full height.

"When you have reached your full height, open the side of the box and set it on the ground. I'll make sure that everyone gets in. I'll be the last one in. Once I get in, you can shut the door and begin our journey," Queen Sharon told Edie.

Edie nodded, and Queen Sharon grabbed her arm just as she lifted the bottle to her lips. "I'm counting on you to keep us safe, Edie. Remember that," the queen told her.

Edie gulped, nodded again, and then drank the potion. The world seemed to shrink around Edie, as her body grew to its normal size. Edie immediately looked down and was surprised to see that since she had been holding the box when she grew, it had grown as well. When Edie had been restored to her full height, she followed Queen Sharon's instructions. She set the open box on the ground, and all the fairies climbed inside. Even though Queen Sharon had already explained how the small box would work, Edie was surprised that almost thirty fairies could fit inside it. Once Queen Sharon had disappeared through the opening, Edie closed and latched the box. Then Edie secured the strap over her shoulder and picked up her backpack.

The sun was resting on the tops of the trees as Edie lifted off from the ground. The box over her arm was much lighter than she had expected. Edie also felt better than she thought she would. She was grateful that she had been able to rest before this flight.

The overcast sky seemed to match Edie's mood. Even though her body was refreshed, her mind was not. Edie tried to push out the doubting thoughts that were creeping into her mind. She knew in the back of her mind that if nothing went wrong, she would be able to make it to Parvack's lair in time to rescue Abbie.

As the sun reached its pinnacle in the sky, Edie decided to stop for a break. She landed lightly on the forest floor and set the box on the ground. Edie tapped lightly on the box and then opened the door in the side. Queen Sharon's head popped over the rim of the box.

"Is it safe to come out?" Queen Sharon asked.

"Yes. I stopped for a break and this part of the forest seems still," Edie replied.

"Very good," said Queen Sharon before she disappeared back into the box.

A few seconds later, Queen Sharon reappeared and flew out of the opening. She looked refreshed and was wearing a beautiful dress that looked like it was made from overlapping green and brown leaves. The rest of the fairies followed her. They flew around, gathering a few nuts and berries to eat. Once they had gotten a small pile, the fairies all gathered around and feasted.

Edie found some food for herself and sat close to the fairies. Unlike the fairies who seemed to be quite enjoying their meal, Edie ate merely to keep up her energy. She was glad when the fairies had finished eating and climbed back in the little wooden box. Edie latched the door and took to the sky to continue her journey.

The skies grew more overcast over the afternoon. Edie scanned the horizon for a sign of storms. Even though the darkened skies threatened to rain, they never followed through.

Edie continued to fly long past nightfall. She battled sleep as she tried to press on just a bit farther. Edie finally grew too tired to fly without danger of going to sleep in the air and falling. So she found a small clearing where she could land.

Edie was so tired that she almost fell as she touched down on the ground. She sleepily knocked on the top of the box and clumsily unlocked the door. Queen Sharon stuck her head out and looked around.

"You've stopped for the night?" Queen Sharon asked.

"Yes," Edie said in mid-yawn.

"Good. Then set the box next to you as you go to sleep and leave the door open a tiny bit. That way no creatures will bother us tonight, but we could get out if we needed too," Queen Sharon said.

"Sure," Edie replied, already half-asleep.

Edie completed the task that Queen Sharon had requested. Then she stretched out on the forest floor. Laying her head down on her knapsack was the last thing Edie remembered before sleep overtook her.

It felt like only minutes before Edie heard someone say her name. She thought at first that it was Abbie trying to wake her up. Then her eyes opened, and she remembered where she was. It was just after sunrise in the forest. The voice Edie had heard belonged to Jem. The fairy had gotten right up next to Edie's ear so that Edie could hear her.

Edie sat up and saw that the rest of the fairies were eating breakfast. As she dug through her knapsack for something to eat, she realized that she had been so weary the night before that she had skipped dinner. When they had all finished their meal, the fairies piled back inside their box, and Edie closed and locked the door behind them. Then Edie took off for Parvack's lair.

Edie was glad that the clear skies held no threat of rain that day. The bright skies allowed her a clear view of the land ahead of her. From where she was, Edie figured that she could make it to Parvack's lair sometime in the middle of the night that night.

By the time she stopped for lunch that day, Edie was quite tired. She was glad to stop for the noontime meal. Edie landed and let the fairies out of their transport box. Queen Sharon flew up so that she could be on eye level with Edie.

"I need an update, Edie. How far do you think we are from Parvack's lair?" Queen Sharon asked.

"I think we should be there some time after dark tonight," Edie answered.

"Very good," Queen Sharon replied. "How are you holding up?"

"I'm tired, but I'll make it. I'll be glad once we're out of Parvack's lair and on the way back home," Edie responded.

"Alright. Just don't push yourself too hard. We don't want you to be too tired to make it back to the Ashcroft Forest," Queen Sharon said.

"I won't. Thank you so much for agreeing to help us," Edie said.

"Absolutely. Once I put myself in your place, there was no way I couldn't help you. Besides, you're the one doing all of the work to get us there," Queen Sharon replied. She then flew back down and joined the other fairies for lunch. Edie and the fairies ate quickly so they could continue their journey.

The afternoon seemed to drag on. Edie was bored flying by herself with only her troubled thoughts to keep her company. As night fell, Edie knew she was getting close to Parvack's lair. Now that Edie knew she could make it to the dragon's lair in time, she began to think about a plan for what they would do when they got there.

Edie was so deep in thought that she almost passed Parvack's cave. She quickly landed about a mile away from his lair and opened the fairies' transport box. Queen Sharon flew out of the box so that she could discuss things with Edie.

"Have we arrived at Parvack's lair?" Queen Sharon asked.

"Yes," replied Edie.

"Good. I'll go back in and get the team that's going to help me lift the spell. If you don't mind, I'll ask you to carry us. That'll help us get to Parvack's cave more quickly," said Queen Sharon before she disappeared into the box. She reappeared just moments later, flanked by four fairies. Edie latched the box per Queen Sharon's order and then the six of them went over their rescue plan. Edie held out her hands, palms up, and the five fairies landed on them. She felt a slight tickling sensation in the middle of her hand as the fairies grabbed her fingers to balance themselves. She fought the urge to laugh aloud and to scratch her hands.

Once the fairies were secure, Edie started down a small hill to Parvack's lair. Edie shivered slightly as she walked. She wasn't really that cold, she was just nervous about dealing with Parvack again. She also had the sudden fear that he might have already eaten Abbie, and she might be leading the fairies into a deadly trap. Edie didn't have long to think about being nervous though, because she had reached the mouth of the cave.

"Parvack!" Edie announced into the cave. "I have returned!"

Chapter Eleven

Dual Freedom

Parvack the dragon lumbered to the cave's entrance. He stopped just short of the edge of the cave. He was so close that Edie could smell his fiery breath. As the dragon stopped, he brought his tail forward. Parvack was holding something limp in the coil at the end of his tail. Edie gasped when she realized the object he was holding was Abbie.

At first, Abbie looked like she was unconscious. Her face was slightly pale, and her wings drooped. Edie's fears were relieved when Abbie's hand moved limply to brush something out of her eye. Edie realized that Abbie was just being still so the dragon wouldn't have a reason to hold her tightly.

"I smell the presence of fairies. You have done well on your mission, Edie," Parvack said looking down at her with eyes devoid of emotion.

"You know the fairies are here. Let Abbie go and then the fairies will lift the curse from you," Edie demanded.

"I don't think so," Parvack replied with a huff and a plume of smoke that Edie assumed was a laugh. "I think I hold the bigger bargaining token. So, I will only release Abbie when I can leave the bounds of my cave."

"Fine then," said Edie. Edie looked down at the fairies holding onto her fingers. She nodded at them to go ahead. The five fairies lifted off Edie's hand and flew the short distance to Parvack. There, they hovered a few inches above his head.

As Edie watched, the fairies cupped their hands and then blew gently into them. Their breath formed into individual spheres of light in their hands. Each of the fairies took their sphere and joined it with Queen Sharon's sphere. Queen Sharon took the large ball of light and flew down to talk to Parvack. What Queen Sharon said to Parvack, Edie didn't know and couldn't hear, but Parvack slowly nodded his large scaly head. Then the dragon opened his mouth, and Queen Sharon placed the glowing sphere on his tongue.

Queen Sharon flew out of Parvack's mouth just in time. Just as Queen Sharon was clear of Parvack's teeth, the dragon closed his mouth with a snap. Nothing happened for a minute. The dragon's eyes suddenly widened. Edie stumbled back several feet, afraid of what would happen next. Parvack's body trembled slightly for a few seconds, and then a small puff of smoke came out of his mouth.

Parvack stood still for a moment before he shook himself all over like a giant dog. He still clutched Abbie in his tail. Dirt and soot fell off of him, and his beautiful scales beamed. He paused for a moment, and Edie wondered what might happen next. Parvack took a few tentative steps toward the edge of the cave. When Parvack stepped over the threshold of the cave, he smiled and released a roar.

"Thank you, Queen Sharon and Edie. You kept your promise to lift the curse from me. Now I will keep my promise and release Abbie," said Parvack. As he said that, Parvack laid his tail on the ground and uncoiled it from around Abbie. Abbie walked forward a few steps and was greeted by a tackling hug from Edie.

"I was so worried about you, Abbie," Edie told her friend as the two of them embraced.

"I was worried about you too, Edie," Abbie replied, relieved to be back with her friend and a little weak from hunger. "I'll tell you all about it when we get home."

"Alright," Edie said nodding. The two of them turned back to face the dragon. Abbie shook herself and swished her knee-length skirt to get the dust and grime off her clothes.

Parvack was stretching his wings experimentally. "It feels so good to be free of that cave," he said in his raspy voice. "Abbie and Edie, I know I only promised you one favor, but if there's anything I can ever help you two with, come find me. Queen Sharon, the same is true for you. If there is ever anything I can help you with, find me and let me know."

"We appreciate that," replied Queen Sharon. Abbie and Edie nodded their agreement.

"Parvack, now that we have completed our transaction, we must go," Edie said.

"Farewell then," Parvack said. "I'm off to find something to eat." His giant teeth gleamed in the sunlight, and Edie shivered at how close she and Abbie had come to being that "something."

With those last words, the dragon leapt into the air and flapped his bat-like wings. Everyone watched as he raised himself into the air and then disappeared over the trees. Even though most creatures fear dragons, they are quite a magnificent sight when they fly.

It was still fairly early in the morning. Edie could hear the forest around her beginning to wake up. The sun was hiding behind the middle of the trees. The sky was clear, and Edie could tell that today was going to be a better day.

Edie held out her hand, and the five fairies flew back and secured themselves on her fingers. She looked over at Abbie. Abbie looked about as tired as Edie felt.

"We've got to go get the rest of the fairies. Come with me," Edie requested.

"Alright," Abbie assented weakly.

They walked back to where Edie had left the fairy transport box. Edie briefly explained the concept of the box to Abbie as Queen Sharon and the four other fairies got back inside. Edie closed the door and locked it. Abbie gathered a few berries to eat as Edie was getting the fairies settled inside the box.

"Are you ready to get back to the Ashcroft Forest?" Edie asked Abbie as Edie slid the box's strap over her arm.

"Absolutely," Abbie replied.

The two sprites ascended over the treetops and headed toward their home. Edie was glad that their journey was almost over. This trip had turned into much more than Edie and Abbie had bargained for when they set out. For the first time in the last four days, Edie wondered how things were going for the sprites in the Ashcroft Forest. A part of her felt bad that she had temporarily forgotten about Mac and the rest of them, but she had focused on rescuing Abbie. It didn't matter though. In rescuing Abbie, Edie had still gotten the fairies on their way to the Ashcroft Forest.

Although Abbie and Edie should have made it back to the Ashcroft Forest by about noon, they were both tired and consequently flew more slowly. Abbie and Edie both got hungry a few hours before they reached the Ashcroft Forest, so they stopped for a short lunch. Edie knocked on the box, and the fairies exited with Queen Sharon to find something to eat. Annie, Becky, and Jordi were relieved and excited to see Abbie. Even though Abbie and Edie both wanted to hear each other's stories, they were more anxious to get back home. Therefore, they talked very little as they ate a quick meal with the fairies and got back on their way.

Edie, Abbie, and the box of fairies reached the Ashcroft Forest sometime in the middle of the afternoon. Edie couldn't have been happier to see familiar surroundings. She stopped at the edge of the village and opened the box that she had used to transport the fairies. Queen Sharon flew out of the box and hovered at Edie's eye level.

"So we have reached the Ashcroft Forest now?" Queen Sharon asked.

"Yes," Edie answered.

"Alright. I'm going to go back and get everyone out so that we can take the growing potion," Queen Sharon replied simply.

"Very good," said Edie.

Queen Sharon flew back down to the box door and called for the fairies to come out. Each of them had a small potion bottle with them. Even though Edie had explained how the transporter worked, Abbie was still surprised at how many fairies came out of the box.

When all of the fairies had gotten out of the box, Edie picked the transporter up. Then the fairies spread out to give themselves room to grow and then drank their potion. Edie and Abbie were soon surrounded by a cluster of fairies the same height that they were.

Annie, Jordi, and Becky surrounded Abbie and gave her a big hug. They all told her how brave they thought she was. Jem stayed close to Queen Sharon, but she gave Abbie a wave when they made eye contact.

Queen Sharon charged Edie with keeping up with the transport box and then asked her to lead the fairies to Fen's house. Edie suddenly felt horrible. In her haste, she had forgotten to tell Queen Sharon about Fen's accident. So after a brief account of Fen's story, Edie and Abbie set off with the group of fairies toward Mac's house. They saw very few sprites on their way. The few that were out looked relieved to see that Abbie and Edie had successfully returned with the fairies. When they reached Mac's house, Abbie walked up and knocked on his door. Mac looked incredibly weary when he opened the door, but visibly brightened when he saw Abbie, Edie, and all of the fairies.

"Thank goodness you're all here!" Mac exclaimed. "I was starting to get really worried about you. I'm glad to see that you made it here safely."

Abbie and Edie exchanged glances at this last comment. If Mac only knew what had happened to them the last few days. Mac, in his excitement, didn't see the look and sigh that passed between the two sprites.

"We don't usually have guests, so we don't have a whole lot of spare beds. We only have two empty guesthouses. I'm sure those of us who escaped the curse wouldn't mind bunking together for a few nights. There are a few beds available in our healing rooms, and we can use Fen's house since he's not using it right now. We'll make this work somehow," Mac rambled, talking quickly.

"Thank you for your hospitality," Queen Sharon said, cutting off Mac's rambling train of thought. "I'm sure that you can work out our sleeping arrangements while we get to work. We'd like to get the healing process started as soon as we can."

"Oh yes! Absolutely!" Mac exclaimed. "Let's get started. Please let me know how we can be of help to you."

"Very good," Queen Sharon replied. "Show us to the first sprite that we can begin to heal."

"OK, let's get started. Abbie and Edie, you both look incredibly tired. Before you go and get some well-deserved rest, would you work out the sleeping arrangements for the fairies?" Mac asked.

"Sure," Edie replied begrudgingly.

Mac led the fairies on a quick tour of the village. He took them to meet Brendon, Kirby, and Walt and then allowed the fairies to set about their work. Meanwhile, Edie and Abbie spent the next hour working out where to house all of the fairies while they were visiting the Ashcroft Forest. Abbie and Edie decided to stay together at Edie's house. They decided that it would make the most sense for the male sprites to stay together in the extra beds in the healing room with Fen. Therefore, the homes of Fen, Brendon, Kirby, Walt, and Abbie would be open to the fairies to stay in. Lenk would remain in Mac's house until he was healed. The rest would stay in the two empty guesthouses. After they had found enough beds for thirty fairies and made arrangements with the owners of the houses that the fairies would be using, Abbie and Edie walked to Edie's house.

As they approached her house, a voice called out behind them. The two of them turned around to see Rufus jogging to catch them. When he reached Abbie, he wrapped her in a tight hug.

"I'm so happy you're home," Rufus told his daughter. "I was so sad that you left before I got a chance to see you the other morning. How did your journey go?"

Abbie recounted the events of the events of the last few days. Even though she tried to skim over the part of her being held hostage by Parvack, Rufus hugged her tightly when she finished. Then he turned and gave Edie a hug too.

"I'm so glad you both made it back safely. You make me so proud," he told them.

"Thanks, dad," Abbie replied.

"Well, I know both of you are tired so I'll see you both later," Rufus said turning away.

"Bye," Abbie and Edie said together.

The two sprites walked into Edie's house and sat down wearily at her kitchen table. They both let out a long sigh and leaned back in their chairs. Neither of them said anything for a moment. Edie was glad for a moment's rest and silence. The silence was short-lived, however, for there was a knock at the door.

Edie pulled herself out of her chair. "What could it be now?" she groaned.

Edie opened the door and was pleasantly surprised to find Michael standing on the other side of it. "I heard that you two had made it home, and I just wanted to come by and check on you," Michael said as he hugged Edie.

Abbie rose from her chair and gave him a hug as well. Abbie and Edie invited Michael to sit down and join them, so that they could talk for a while. Even though she was extremely tired, Edie was excited to be able to finally hear Michael and Abbie's stories from the last few days. Frankly, she was glad to have someone to talk to at all. The last four days had been rather lonely for her.

Chapter Twelve

The Curse Is Lifted

Michael sat down at Edie's kitchen table. He politely asked about Abbie and Edie's trip to Holli Lake. Edie knew that Michael probably expected to receive an uneventful trip report, and she bet that he would be surprised to hear that Parvack had held Abbie as a hostage. Michael didn't disappoint Edie. He was shocked when Edie told him about the first part of their trip.

"Are you alright?" Michael asked, turning to Abbie and touching her arm.

"Yeah," Abbie replied, nodding her head. "I was very relieved when Edie got back with the fairies though. I will save my part of the story for later. I want to hear Edie's part first."

Edie obliged Abbie and proceeded to tell about the part of the journey after Edie had left Parvack's cave. Both Abbie and Michael were extremely thankful that Queen Sharon had changed her mind about rescuing Abbie. They were also glad that Edie had managed to reach Parvack's lair before sunrise. Michael was amazed that all the fairies had arrived in the Ashcroft Forest when Edie showed him the box that she had used to transport the fairies. When Edie reached the point of the story where she and the fairies arrived at Parvack's lair, she got Abbie to help her fill in the details of the rest of the story.

"I do have a question for you, Edie," Abbie stated.

"Yes?" Edie replied.

"Why did Queen Sharon have to put the glowing ball inside Parvack's mouth?" Abbie asked.

"I asked that same question of Queen Sharon when we were going over the plan of how to rescue you. She told me that in order for a creature to have a curse lifted, the evil inside the creature from the curse has to be cleaned out first. Once the inside is clean, the outside can be cleaned. That's why once Parvack had swallowed the ball of light, all the dust and dirt fell off him," Edie answered. Abbie nodded along with that explanation.

Edie continued, "Queen Sharon told me that that is how Jem lifted my curse. She couldn't clean out the cursed part of me all at once, however, because I'm not as strong as Parvack. She had to do it little pieces at the time.

"Ah, that makes sense now. I wondered how those little glowing balls were going to cure you," Abbie said with a chuckle to herself as she sorted everything out.

"Right. So what happened to you while you were in Parvack's cave?" Edie asked Abbie.

"I'm not going to lie. I was incredibly scared the whole time I was there. My heart sank as I watched you fly away. Knowing how fickle dragons are, I was worried that Parvack would change his mind and eat me before you got back, Edie. I had faith that you could make it back in time though," Abbie said evenly despite her fear at the memory.

"What did you do for the four days you were in the dragon's cave?" Michael asked.

"Right after you left, Parvack asked me what I could do to entertain him. He said that I would have to keep him occupied to keep his mind off his hunger. I told him that I could tell stories, and that I could sing. I talked and sang to him almost the entire four days. The few times that Parvack let me stop to rest, I fell into a troubled sleep because I was so worried that he would eat me while I was asleep. To begin with, I made up most of the stories that I told him. I didn't want to tell him anything about the Ashcroft Forest. After two or three days with no sleep and only the little bit of food and water in my knapsack, I began to lose faith. So, I filled my mind with thoughts of the Ashcroft Forest and of both of you. Consequently, the plots of my stories became more real as I began to relay stories of my life. It was the only way I could keep my hopes of coming home alive," Abbie replied, almost in tears by the end of her story.

"You must be tired then," Edie said.

"I am," Abbie said with a noise that Edie wasn't sure was a sob or a yawn, "but I want to hear what happened to Michael while we were gone."

"Nothing very interesting went on around here. We went about our usual activities during the day. Then around sunset, Walt locked us in. I don't remember much of what happened during the night, but I know that Mac, Kirby, Walt, and Brendon made sure we didn't get out of our houses. Rufus, Wayne, and Walt must have made incredibly strong locks because none of us escaped. Even though Joneé has helped him as much as she can, Mac has grown more and more tired from stress and anxiety each day. I'm glad that the two of you got back when you did. I feel bad that all of this had to happen at once," Michael replied.

Abbie and Edie both nodded. "Has anything changed with Fen's condition?" Abbie asked.

Michael's expression became grimmer. "I'm afraid not. Nothing has changed while you were gone. Lenk said there isn't a whole lot he can do to bring Fen back to consciousness. He has remedies to heal Fen's broken limbs, but he doesn't have a way to make him conscious again," Michael answered.

"Well, we'll just have to support Mac all we can," Edie said firmly.

"Absolutely," Michael and Abbie agreed.

"I think Abbie and I both need sleep before we do anything else, however. Michael, the fairies are probably looking for you so that they can begin your healing process," Edie said.

"Oh, right," Michael replied as he stood up from the table. "I'll leave you two to get some rest. I'm glad that you got home safely. See you soon."

Abbie and Edie walked Michael to the door, and both gave him a hug. They watched him sprint over to his house, and then Edie closed the door. Edie noticed that Abbie had a thoughtful look on her face.

"What are you thinking about?" Edie asked her.

"I'm just surprised that none of the sprites we've seen so far have shown outward characteristics of the curse. None of them look like animals yet. I'm glad, because that'll make it easier for the fairies to lift the curse. The hardest part of your recovery was having to re-grow your wings," Abbie explained.

Edie nodded and yawned. "Yes, hopefully it'll be easier on them than it was for me. I'm glad I was unconscious for the early stages of my healing," Edie said.

Abbie caught Edie's yawn, and she decided that it was time for a well-deserved nap. Abbie gathered her things and began to make a bed out of Edie's couch. However, since Abbie had lost so much sleep, Edie volunteered to sleep on the couch instead. Abbie didn't argue, so they both went to their respective beds and fell asleep.

Despite sleeping on a couch, Edie slept soundly through the afternoon and night. She awoke refreshed the next morning. Edie tiptoed into the room where Abbie was sleeping to see if she was still asleep. After seeing that Abbie was indeed still sleeping, Edie slipped outside and went to look for Michael. Queen Sharon was just exiting the house across from Abbie's house.

Edie called out to the fairy and walked toward her. "Queen Sharon!" Edie called softly.

Queen Sharon turned around and waited for Edie to catch up. "How are things going so far?" Edie asked when she caught up to her.

"We got here before the curse was able to take much of a hold on your friends. We should be able to have the curse lifted off the sprites by the day after tomorrow. Then we'll be able to focus on looking for the fairy that caused all this trouble in the first place," Queen Sharon answered.

"You think they'll be healed that quickly? That's great!" Edie exclaimed. "I'll let you get back to what you were doing then."

"Alright, Edie, I'll see you soon," Queen Sharon said as she walked to Joneé's house.

Edie turned the opposite direction and walked the short distance to Michael's house. She knocked gently on his door. Michael cautiously opened the door, but he smiled when he saw who was paying him a visit. He asked her to come in and have some breakfast with him.

"I was just beginning to wonder if you two were awake," Michael said as he closed the door behind Edie. "Was Abbie up when you left your house?"

"No, and I just figured I'd let her sleep," Edie answered.

"That's probably the best idea," Michael replied.

"Queen Sharon said that the fairies should be able to lift the curse from you completely by the day after tomorrow," Edie told Michael.

"That's wonderful!" Michael exclaimed.

There was a brief silence as Michael seemed lost in thought. "Michael!" Edie said suddenly, interrupting his thoughts.

"Yes?" he asked in surprise.

"I've just thought of something. Are Wayne and Trista alright?" Edie asked.

"Yes. We locked Wayne and Trista in separate bedrooms, so that they wouldn't have to worry about Trista getting hurt. Like I said before, the locks that Wayne, Rufus, and Walt put on were incredibly strong," Michael told her.

"That's good," Edie replied.

The two of them continued to talk as they finished their meal. Just as they finished eating, there was a knock on the door. Michael walked over and opened it. Abbie was waiting on the other side of the door. Michael gave her a big hug and invited her to come in.

As Michael made breakfast for Abbie, Edie updated Abbie on what Queen Sharon had told her. Abbie was quite excited to hear Queen Sharon's news. She would be glad when all of this trouble would be over, and things could go back to normal. Well, as normal as things could be while Fen was unconscious.

The next two days passed quickly. As Queen Sharon had promised earlier, the fairies rid the sprites of their curse by the end of the second day. All the sprites were relieved to be free of their animal curse. They immediately began to clean up the damage that their night transformations had caused. Wayne, Rufus, and Walt went around and removed all of the locks from the houses.

During those two days, Queen Sharon and Mac discussed ways the fairies could go search for the renegade fairy. On the morning of the third day, the fairies split up into a few groups and went in search of the fairy that had spread the curse. The plan was that the fairies would search during the day, and then come back to the village to sleep at night. When one of the groups found the evil fairy, they would bring it back to the village at once. What Queen Sharon would do with the fairy once they had captured it, no one knew except her.

Chapter Thirteen

Capture

The fairies left on their search early each morning and got back late each night. The first few days, the fairies were quite eager to begin their search. As the days dragged on, however, the fairies grew more and more tired. After several days, the fairies began to grow weary from their journeys and frustrated that they hadn't found the missing fairy.

The sprites volunteered to go out on some of the searches, but the fairies had politely turned down their offer. Queen Sharon had explained that it would probably be more dangerous to have a sprite join their scouting parties. She recommended that the sprites stay indoors as much as they could. That way they wouldn't run the risk of being cursed again if the fairy returned.

The sprites heeded Queen Sharon's advice. They stayed in their homes in the village as much as possible. In the evening, they looked after the fairies by cooking for them when they came back from their daily excursions.

Abbie rarely got to see the friends she had made while she had been at Holli Lake. Becky, Annie, and Jordi were gone every day searching for the fairy. After making sure that all of the sprites had returned to their normal selves and setting everything up for healing the fairy once it had been found, Jem decided to join the search parties too. Edie and Abbie would occasionally see one of their friends and wave, but the fairies were always busy and tired.

After thirteen long days of searching, Queen Sharon decided that the fairies needed to change their search strategy. She went to the house where she had been staying and crafted four bottles of shrinking potion and five bottles of growing potions. Queen Sharon selected four of her fairies and directed them to take the shrinking potion the next morning. Then they would be the same size as the fairy they were looking for. She hoped that possibly being the same size would give those fairies an advantage in finding the fairy they were searching for.

Thinking optimistically, Queen Sharon instructed the fairies that the extra growing potion was to be given to the fairy once they captured him or her so that it would be easier for them to bring the fairy back to the village. The remaining fairies would still go searching the next morning, but they would remain sprite height.

Edie realized after a few days that she had neglected to ask about the fairy. She was sure that Queen Sharon knew exactly which fairy it was, but she had never even asked whether the fairy was male or female. At this point, Edie felt too embarrassed to ask any of the fairies, so she decided to ask Abbie.

It had been almost three weeks since the fairies had arrived in the Ashcroft Forest. Edie, Michael, and Abbie were sitting at Michael's kitchen table having lunch. They had made themselves some strawberry jam sandwiches.

"Abbie, do you know anything about the fairy they are searching for?" Edie asked her friend.

"I don't know much about him, Edie," she replied. "I know that his name is Charlie and that something awful happened right before he left Holli Lake. I don't really know anything other than that."

"That's more than I knew," Michael said as he cleared his mouth of food. "I wasn't even sure if the fairy was a boy or a girl." Edie gave a small giggle, feeling better that she wasn't alone in not knowing. Abbie looked at both of them quizzically.

They munched in silence for a moment before they heard a commotion right outside. The three of them walked to the door and stepped out so that they could get a better look at what was going on.

When Edie stepped outside, she saw that several other sprites were standing outside their homes trying to get a look at the source of the commotion. The noise came from a group of fairies that were slowly making their way down the path to Mac's house. Four fairies, whose names Edie remembered to be David, Noble, Liz, and James, were holding tightly to another fairy who was struggling violently. Although the fifth fairy's wrists and ankles were bound, the fairy still fought hard for freedom.

Edie immediately knew that the struggling fairy she saw before her was the one for whom the fairies had been searching, Charlie. This fairy looked so much different from the other fairies that Edie had been around. The male fairy had black hair that had grown long and tangled since he had left Holli Lake. His wings had turned jet black, and he had lost the glow that all of the other fairies had. His clothes were similar to the other fairies, but they had grown worn and ragged. However, the scariest thing about the renegade fairy was his eyes. The inner part of the evil fairy's eyes had turned onyx, and the two eyes flicked back and forth wildly.

Despite the fairy's frightening appearance, a feeling of relief swept over Edie. She knew that it would be a bit difficult for everyone while Queen Sharon figured out what to do with the trouble-making fairy. Soon, however, things in the Ashcroft Forest would be back to normal. Edie would be quite thankful for a bit of peace and quiet in their little village.

Edie's attention returned to the scene in front of her as the small group of fairies reached Mac's door. Liz, Noble, and James held the straining fairy just long enough for David to knock on Mac's front door. Mac quickly opened the door, already fully dressed, and his eyes widened at the sight in front of him. Even though the group of fairies had stopped walking, the cursed fairy continued to struggle and yell.

Mac immediately took control of the situation. He asked the sprites that were watching the fairies to return to their normal activities. He then set about finding a place to hold the renegade fairy until Queen Sharon could decide the best thing to do with him. They put Charlie in a room off the meeting hall. Lenk gave the fairy some food with a sleeping potion in it so that the fairy would not be able to cause any more trouble until Queen Sharon returned. David, Noble, Liz, and James stood guard outside the room until Queen Sharon returned that night.

Michael, Edie, and Abbie walked back into the house and finished their jam sandwiches. Michael and Abbie were quite relieved that Charlie had been caught. They were interested to see what had caused him to turn so evil.

"Did you see his eyes?" Abbie asked Michael and Edie while they were finishing their sandwiches.

Both sprites nodded, and Edie shuddered at the memory. "I wonder what could have happened to him," she said in a hushed whisper.

Mac met each of the fairy search groups when they returned to the Ashcroft Forest. As soon as they heard that the fairy had been captured, they went to see how they could help rehabilitate him. Queen Sharon's group was the last group to come back that night. She was glad to hear that the hunt for the missing fairy was finally over.

All of the sprites were anxious to see what would happen. They waited expectantly the first day to hear what was going on. The only time the sprites saw the fairies was when the fairies occasionally ventured out to get food. The rest of the time, they stayed together in the room off the meeting hall, presumably trying to heal the misguided fairy. Edie wanted to pull one of them off to the side to see what had happened, but she knew she would be interrupting the work they were doing. Three days after David, Noble, Liz, and James had captured the fairy, Mac and Queen Sharon finally called a meeting. By that time, the sprites' curiosity was almost to the breaking point.

Chapter Fourteen

Charlie

When Abbie, Michael, and Edie arrived at the meeting hall, the sprites were buzzing with excitement. They had all made theories about what happened to the fairy to cause his personality to become so dark, but now they would finally know the truth.

After all of the sprites had come in and taken a seat, Mac, Joneé, Queen Sharon, and all of the fairies walked in from the back of the hall and down to the front of the room. They all had a seat, and Mac called the meeting to order. The sprites in the room immediately fell silent so that they could hear what was going on. Once everyone was quiet, Mac allowed Queen Sharon to take control of the meeting.

"Thank you all for coming," Queen Sharon started, rising from her chair. She looked well put together as always, and her short greying hair was set off with a red holly berry in it. It matched her long berry red dress that cinched at the waist and flowed down to her ankles. She was elegant, yet formidable as always.

"As you know, three days ago David, Noble, Liz, and James found the fairy that has caused us all so much trouble," Queen Sharon continued. "I'm very grateful to them for having found him."

The sprites gave the four fairies a polite round of applause. Queen Sharon continued, "The fairies and I have spent the last three days working to heal and rehabilitate this fairy. Our efforts have been successful, and today this fairy is back to normal. We called this meeting today to give him an opportunity to speak to you and apologize for all the trouble he has caused. So I'm going to ask Charlie to come up and speak to you at this time."

Queen Sharon sat back down, and a handsome young fairy walked onto the platform. Edie almost didn't recognize him. Charlie looked so different from the angry fairy that had been dragged into the village three days earlier. All sense of darkness had left him. His dark hair had been cut short, and his eyes had turned a soft brown color. The fairy glow had returned to his body, and his wings had become white and glittering.

Charlie seemed to be a bit intimidated by the gathering of sprites, but he gathered his courage and began to speak. "Hi everyone," Charlie began by giving a small awkward wave. "I want to apologize for all the trouble I've caused all of you. A few months ago I was out with my best friend, Max. The two of us had been sent to get twigs and pine bark so that the carpenter could make a few more tables for our dining hall. A few of the tables had gotten worn out, and he wanted to replace them. So my friend and I, excited to get some fresh air, were glad to be of assistance."

"Max picked up the limbs, and I picked up the bark. Once we had gotten all that we needed, the two of us walked back to the entrance to our home because our loads were too heavy to be able to fly. We were almost home when Max tripped over something and fell."

At the end of the last sentence, Charlie seemed to choke up a bit. He shook his head as if to clear away the emotion, and then continued, "When Max stood up, he had a huge gash on his face. Being a very clumsy person myself, I happened to have a bottle in my pocket that contained a solution that would heal cuts and things in fairies. So I quickly pulled it out of my pocket and applied a bit of it to the wound. My friend thanked me for my quick thinking and then asked me what the stuff was that I had put on his cut. When I told him what it was, his eyes grew very large and round.

"'Charlie, please tell me you didn't put that on my cut!' Max begged, fear in his eyes.

"'Of course I did, mate. It's some of the best medicine for healing fairy cuts. Why do you have that look on your face?' I replied.

"'Charlie, I'm allergic to that. I've got to get to Jem quickly. I could die from something like that!' he yelped.

"So the two of us flew toward the shelter. His face was swelling rapidly, and he collapsed just as we reached the entrance. I picked him up and carried him in, yelling for help and for someone to get Jem.

"By the time I finally found Jem, my friend's breathing was shallow. I quickly explained what happened, and Jem assessed his condition. She tried her best to save him, but too much time had passed for her to be able to stop the effects of the medicine I had given him.”

At that point, Charlie broke down in tears for a moment. A few of the fairies moved toward him, but he waved them off and regained his composure. Charlie continued, “I was so upset that I flew to my room and cried until sleep overtook me. I awoke to the sound of someone knocking on my door. I opened the door to see who it was. Two guards stood outside. They told me that they had a few questions for me. They asked me to describe the accident and what happened afterward. I noticed that the two guards were exchanging strange glances while I was telling my story.

“When I finished, one of the guards looked at me and said this: ‘That’s a good story Charlie. However, do you expect us to believe that you were friends with this fairy all this time, and you didn’t know that he was allergic to that medicine? Something isn’t right about that. It sounds to me that you were looking for a way to get rid of your competition.’

“‘What!?’ I yelled. These guards were crazy! How could they think that I killed my best friend?

“‘We all know that you and your friend were both signed up to compete in the race next week. There’s been a lot of stress on both of you, so we didn’t know if that would give you reason to want to get your friend out of the way so that he couldn’t race with you,’ the guard had replied.

“I told them I had no idea what they were talking about. The two guards had told me that they would report the incident to Queen Sharon, let her decide what to do, and then come back for me. I sat there for a moment after they left, shocked by what they thought I had done. Then a strangely wonderful idea came to me. I could run away. Run away from fairies who believed that I could commit such a crime. Run away from the horrible tragedy I had seen earlier that day. Run away and not have to deal with consequences of a crime I hadn’t committed. So I quickly gathered a few of my belongings and fled.

“So I turned my back on Holli Lake and set off by myself. The farther I went, the more I began to blame myself for what had happened to my friend. It felt like a dark shadow was following me everywhere I went. My grief didn’t last though because I soon grew angry about the incident. By the time I neared Parvack's lair, my anger had consumed me. I couldn't hold it back any longer. So I laid my first curse on Parvack, the dragon. It felt good getting rid of my anger as I was weaving the curse over him. I immediately felt bad about what I had done, however, so I fled.

"I promised myself that I wouldn't try to harm anyone else. I would remain in the clearing just outside the village here because placing the curse on Parvack took a lot out of me. I watched all of you go about your daily lives, while I regained my strength. I was lonely and wished that my best friend were with me. I began to grow depressed watching all of you. You all seemed so happy. The seed of bitterness and rage I had been carrying grew stronger with every happy sprite that I saw. I vowed that I would take out my anger on the next sprite that came through the clearing. Edie, you unfortunately were the next sprite who came my way. So I took out my anger on you.

"Again, releasing my rage felt good as I was casting the spell. After I cast the spell on Edie, I felt bad again. I wanted to be done with all the sadness and anger. A few weeks later, though, I saw you all gathering for your monthly celebration. I couldn't understand why the sprites I saw before me could be so happy when I was so miserable. So I laid my biggest curse yet. I thought maybe a bigger curse would help me to feel better. After I had done it, I felt none of the fulfillment I had expected. I had expected to feel better, but I felt the worst I had since I left my home.

So I went off by myself for a while. I didn't go far, because I was so exhausted I could hardly move. But I didn't want to get close again so I wouldn't have to see your suffering under the curse or see you happy as you went about your day. I toiled away my days in a nearby field, as sad and lonely as ever. I barely ate because I was so upset.

"One day, I was out in a nearby field picking a few berries so that I wouldn't starve. The next thing I knew, two sets of arms had grabbed me from behind, and the other two were tying my arms and legs. I immediately recognized them as the four fairies sitting here in front of me and knew they would try to take me back to Holli Lake. I didn't want to go back though. All the way back to the Ashcroft Forest, I struggled with them and begged them to let me go. They managed, despite my fiercest efforts, to get me here and give me treatment. For that, I am extremely grateful to them.

"The fairies have helped me release my anger. I've not just pushed it down so that it can be ignored and resurface. But I've given it up completely so that it can't come back to harm me or anyone else. Queen Sharon has assured me that she doesn't hold me responsible for what happened to Max. She understands that it was an accident.

"However, I am responsible for what I did to you. I want to apologize to all of you for my behavior the last few months. In addition, I'd like to thank all of you for your hospitality. Jem and Queen Sharon have told me that they have successfully completed my treatment. We will be leaving tomorrow morning to return to Holli Lake. I think that's all I have to say, except to tell you all thank you once again."

With that, Charlie sat down again and gave a visible sigh of relief. Several of the fairies around him patted him on the back. Jordi, who was sitting next to him, grabbed his hand and squeezed it. She sat there holding it the rest of the time they were in the room. The assembled sprites and fairies gave him a round of applause. Mac stood up and waited for things to quiet down again.

"We're going to adjourn the meeting now, but feel free to stay around in the meeting hall to talk. The fairies will be going home tomorrow, so make sure to say your goodbyes," Mac told the group.

Some of the sprites began to trickle out. Abbie, Edie, and Michael stayed around and talked with the fairies for a few minutes. Becky, Annie, Jordi, and Jem were all relieved that the search was over and that they would soon be going home. Edie felt sad that the fairies would be going home, but the fairies invited Edie, Abbie, and Michael to visit whenever they wanted. Then they asked Mac and Queen Sharon if there was anything they could do to get the fairies ready to depart the next morning.

"There's nothing you can really do today. After the fairies leave tomorrow, I know of something you could do to help me. I would appreciate it if you would clean the homes that the fairies used. Then we can begin to get things back to normal," Mac answered.

"Alright," Michael, Edie, and Abbie agreed.

Before they left, Edie got the attention of Queen Sharon. "Queen Sharon?" Edie asked as she walked closer to her.

"Yes, Edie?" Queen Sharon responded.

"I have a question for you," Edie said. Queen Sharon nodded for her to continue. "Is there anything you can do for Fen?"

Queen Sharon pursed her lips. "Jem has done what she could for him. She has healed his wounds and wings. But unfortunately, there is nothing she can do to bring him back to consciousness. She's given Lenk some things he can try to help him. Other than that, you all will just have to wait and see," Queen Sharon said, lifting her shoulders slightly.

Edie nodded. "Thank you, Queen Sharon. I appreciate all of the help that you have given us," she said.

"You're welcome, Edie," Queen Sharon replied. "I'm sorry there isn't more I could do to help Fen."

The three sprites headed back to their houses. They all went to bed early, knowing that they would have to get up early the next morning in order to see the fairies depart. Edie sighed as she climbed into bed. She was glad to think that after tomorrow, things would be getting back to normal around the Ashcroft Forest.

Chapter Fifteen

Jay

The next morning, Edie, Michael, and Abbie woke up in time to see the fairies before they departed. Edie made sure to give Queen Sharon her transport box back. The three of them had spent so much time with the fairies that it was difficult to see them leave, but Queen Sharon told them that they would be welcome guests in her kingdom anytime. Edie and Abbie found Becky, Annie, and Jordi and told the three young fairies goodbye. All three were too tired for any tears, but they made Edie and Abbie promise to come visit Holli Lake soon.

Gaining the attention of her fairies, Queen Sharon told them it was time to leave. The sprites hugged the fairies and bid them farewell. As the assembled sprites watched, the fairies flew off in the direction of Holli Lake. The fairies would wait until they reached Holli Lake to shrink to their normal size since they had used all but one of the extra shrinking potions that they had brought with them. It would make their journey shorter if they remained at their larger height.

Edie, Abbie, and Michael spent most of the morning cleaning the houses that the fairies had used. The fairies weren't necessarily messy, but Michael, Edie, and Abbie just wanted to make things tidy for their original residents. By that night, all three of them were exhausted and sore. They all headed to their own houses and slept peacefully for the first time in quite a while.

The next week went by uneventfully. Everyone was glad to go back to their normal lives, free from the twists and turns that the last weeks had taken. With things in the Ashcroft Forest slowing down, Joneé and Mac were able to take a well-deserved break and get some rest. Lenk continued to treat Fen, though he remained unconscious.

The following week began with the celebration of the eighth of the month. Since the fairies had lifted the curse and healed Charlie, there was a lot for the sprites to celebrate. All of the sprites prepared for this celebration eagerly. The celebration lasted long into the night, as always. Everyone enjoyed being able to relax and have fun together.

The next day, Edie, Michael, and Abbie slept late and then went to gather food together. When they arrived back in the village, Michael offered to make a late lunch for the three of them. Edie and Abbie accepted his offer but went home first to put their own food away.

As Edie and Abbie were walking back to Michael's house, a sprite that they had never seen before stumbled out of the woods, taking them both by surprise. The sprite looked as though he hadn't slept or bathed in several days. His ear-length blonde hair was slightly matted, his arms and legs had several cuts and bruises, and his clothes were tattered. The sprite's blue eyes held a look of despair and fear, and his forest-green wings seemed to droop. He looked at Abbie and Edie and seemed momentarily speechless.

"Hi?" Abbie said gently. Although the sprite looked a bit frightening, he didn't seem like a threat. He just looked lost.

"Are you looking for someone?" she asked.

"I'm looking for my family," the sprite replied.

"Oh, I see," Abbie replied, trying to think of something else to say. She looked at Edie, who seemed at as much of a loss for words as the mystery sprite. "What's your name?"

"Jay," the sprite answered.

"Alright, Jay. This is my friend Edie," Abbie said pointing to Edie. "We'll take you to visit our village leaders, Mac and Joneé, and see if they know your family. Would you like something to eat first?"

Jay's eye brightened, and he nodded hungrily.

"Then follow us. We're going to have lunch with our friend," she told him.

Jay followed Abbie and Edie to Michael's house. Since Michael knew they were coming, Abbie opened the door and walked in. Michael had already set the table for three.

"Michael, we've brought someone with us to lunch. I hope that's alright," Abbie called.

"You should have told me you were bringing someone else to lunch. I've only set three places," Michael replied from the kitchen in a slightly grumpy tone. He walked out and set another place without looking up.

"I'm sorry," Abbie apologized. "Michael, this is Jay. We found him outside, and he said he's looking for his family. He looked really hungry so we thought we'd bring him in before we took him to meet Mac and Joneé..."

Abbie trailed off at the look on Jay's face. Edie had noticed it too and was looking at him questioningly. Michael walked back toward the kitchen to get the food that he had prepared.

"What were you saying, Abbie?" Michael asked her.

"Michael?" Jay asked looking at him hopefully.

Michael turned around to look at the sprite who had addressed him. An odd look spread across his face. In that one expression, Edie knew that Michael recognized Jay from his past and that Michael's lost memories were coming back to him. She also sensed that the peace and rest she had enjoyed the last few days had ended.

End.